Excess

Excess

THE KNOTTING HILL OMEGAVERSE

COLETTE RHODES

ISBN 978-1-7386107-5-4 (paperback)

ISBN 978-1-7386107-6-1 (hardcover)

CONTENT WARNING

WHAT IS OMEGAVERSE?

WHILE THERE ARE MANY DIFFERENT INTERPRETATIONS OF "OMEGAVERSE" IN FICTION (AND THIS ONE HAS A FEW QUIRKS OF ITS OWN), THE BASIC CONCEPT IS A DOMINANCE HIERARCHY AMONG HUMANS WHEREBY EVERYONE IS EITHER BORN AN ALPHA, A BETA, OR AN OMEGA. A PERSON'S DESIGNATION IMPACTS THEIR PLACE IN SOCIETY, AS WELL AS THEIR ROMANTIC AND SEXUAL RELATIONSHIPS.

OMEGAVERSE INCLUDES KNOTTING, HEATS, SCENT MARKING, AND OTHER ANIMALISTIC BEHAVIOURS.

IN THIS WORLD, OMEGAS CAN ONLY BE CLAIMED VIA MATING BITE DURING THEIR HEAT. TO BITE THEM AT ANY OTHER TIME IS FATAL TO THE ALPHA.

AUTHOR'S NOTE

WHILE I USUALLY WRITE IN US ENGLISH, THE ON THE SHELF SERIES IS SET IN THE UK, AND I COULDN'T IN GOOD CONSCIOUS HAVE A BRITISH CHARACTER SAY "MOM", SO THIS BOOK IS WRITTEN IN BRITISH ENGLISH.

IF YOU'RE WORRIED THAT MY BRITISH ENGLISH WILL BE WORSE THAN MY AMERICAN ENGLISH, PLEASE REST ASSURED THAT I AM FROM NEW ZEALAND AND PROBABLY UNFIT TO WRITE BOTH.

"Fuck! Is one expected to be a gentleman when one is stiff?"
—Marquis de Sade

Chapter 1

INIKA

"What are your plans for your heat?" Maia asked with discomfiting familiarity, lounging in the chair in front of my desk and taking notes at rapid-fire pace on her phone. "It's coming up, no?"

"It is. It's really not considered good form to ask about it, though."

She shrugged, unapologetic. Maia's no-nonsense approach to everything was why I'd hired her as my assistant in the first place, but it had its drawbacks. Then again, perhaps all betas would be as blasé about such a topic? The concept of heats was as foreign to them as the concept of casual dating was to me.

"I mean, I need to know how accessible you're going to be," she retorted, tossing her inky black hair over her shoulder and raising a pierced eyebrow at me. "I know you've put in notice to go on leave, but the office might still reach out. I need to know what to tell them."

"How much experience do you have with omegas in heat?" I asked, amused. "I will be entirely inaccessible. Negative accessible. If you attempt to speak to me, I may claw your eyeballs out of your face, and I wouldn't even realise I'd done it until after I'd emerged from my nest."

Maia's other eyebrow shot up. "That feral, huh? Sounds like a pain."

"Something like that," I agreed. "You'll need to block off five days on the calendar from when my heat hits—at the very minimum. I've already given the team an approximate date, and it's an annual event so they know what to expect from me, but if you could confirm with them that I'm no longer available when I retreat to my nest, that would be great. You'll also need to contact Prendre and ask them to send the alpha over if I don't manage to contact them before I lose my senses."

Maia glanced up from her furious note-taking, her eyebrows shooting up. "The *what*?"

I'd never had to explain any of this to Tess, my previous assistant. But I supposed I couldn't hold it against her that she wanted to go off and see the world rather than being cooped up in my house most of the day, stuck doing my bidding. The compensation was generous, but it probably wasn't the glamorous role she'd envisioned as an heiress's personal assistant.

Maia disliked people and rarely left the staff accommodation at the back of the property when she wasn't working. We were a much better fit. She also only answered to me—unlike Tess, who'd been hired by my parents.

"The alpha," I repeated with a wry smile. "Not *my* alpha. Prendre is an agency that connects alphas who... make themselves available, with single omegas for their heats."

"Like a gigolo or something?"

"It's not quite as involved as all that," I laughed. Well, there probably *were* alphas who operated more as kept lovers, but I had no interest in one of those. "There's an interview process beforehand which I'll need to set in motion shortly. I select who I want, they appear for the heat, then they disappear again afterwards. There are nests-for-hire available on their premises, but I use the spare bedroom as a temporary nest. Obviously, I wouldn't bring them back to my real one."

"Obviously," Maia repeated faintly. "Couldn't they just bite you, though? When you're not poisonous?"

It was a distasteful topic of conversation, but I didn't shut it down. Not everyone was as non-judgemental about my use of alphas-for-hire as Maia appeared to be.

Actually, it was quite nice to be asked. Mostly, people decided they already knew everything about how omegas worked. Half the time, they were alpha-splaining it to me.

"The toxin in my blood is neutralised during my heat, so they *could* bite me without suffering any harm. Which is why there are... muzzles involved." I did blush at that, imagining the visual that Maia would come up with. It was just as sordid as it sounded. "Mated alphas stand guard outside around the clock. The working alpha takes food and water breaks when the omega sleeps; the guards are mostly there to see to their needs."

There was nothing more resilient than an omega in heat. I didn't need food. I survived on electrolyte drinks sucked through a straw. What I *needed* was orgasms.

Maia blinked. "Wow. That all sounds... elaborate."

"It is. It's not a realistic option for most omegas." We both knew I wasn't most omegas when it came to finances.

"I have a lot more questions."

I tried and failed to suppress a smile. "You can ask one. I probably need to start getting ready for tonight."

By which I meant I would take off my make-up, put on a sheet mask, and lie in my nest to disassociate for as long as physically possible before *actually* getting ready.

Maia mulled it over, drumming the back of her phone case with her pointed nails. "I was going to ask if it wouldn't just be easier to get a mate, but I guess I know the answer to that. That's a very permanent decision that you have to live with outside the nest, too."

"It is." A very permanent decision for a very indecisive omega to make.

"Okay. Okay, here's my question. Is it a taboo thing? I don't mean that as an insult or anything, but if I hired someone to bang me for several days—*with a muzzle on, no less*—I think I'd, you know, get some looks. At the very least."

"I've never considered that," I laughed. Most of my staff and my colleagues were betas. It wasn't like I didn't spend time around them. But sometimes I forgot their *needs* were so different from mine. So easily managed and unobtrusive. "The agencies aren't considered taboo, per se. They're not only used for heats, and it's a luxury experience, so there's a sense of... exclusivity about it, I suppose."

I hesitated, choosing my words carefully. "That they service omegas in heat is probably seen as taboo by some people. It's not a particularly well-known practice outside of, well, those who can afford it, I suppose."

Maia nodded thoughtfully. "My mam would probably have a heart attack if I told her about it. Which I won't, obviously. She'd definitely say it was rich people nonsense, though."

"It's absolutely rich people nonsense," I agreed. I suspected even more of my life was rich people nonsense than I realised.

"Do you need anything else from me before I head out?" Maia asked. "Need me to call that agency or whatever for you?"

My lips twitched. "No, I can manage that on my own. Thank you."

I recognised that I was out of touch by most people's standards, but it would be a truly grim day when I outsourced the coordination of my sex appointments.

"Very good." Maia stood, grabbing the textured leather tote bag I'd bought her for her birthday from the empty chair next to her and tucking her phone into the inside pocket. "Oh, I meant to tell you that I finally heard back from that plasterer this morning. Blake what's-his-face." She wrinkled her nose. "He's a rude prick, if I'm being completely honest. He had a last-minute cancellation so I guess he can fit you in. He wants to come around tomorrow and see the space. What do you want me to tell him? You're free until midday, though I'm guessing tonight is going to be a late night."

I hummed in agreement, immediately feeling flat at the reminder of tonight's event. "It'll be fine. I don't intend on staying out late. Tell him he can come first thing and I'll show him the space. Let's see if this guy lives up to the hype."

"Inika! There you are," Mama said, grabbing my hands with her slightly shaky ones and giving them a light squeeze as she kissed the air next to my cheek. "You're late, my darling."

"Fashionably so," I replied airily, rather than telling her that I'd had to unwillingly drag myself out from the depths of my nest and force myself into this skintight silk dress at the last possible minute.

"The awards haven't started yet, at least." Mama's smile was tight, the scent of omega distress permeating the air. Not for long, though. She'd excuse herself to slather on one of the many tubes of Om-Guard she had in her clutch. I suspected there were a few medically prescribed goodies in there designed to keep her calm too, but she'd never admit to it.

"Papa would have been upset if you'd missed his moment. It's your moment too, you know. Our moment, as a family." She squeezed my fingers once more before releasing me. "You're his legacy."

"I wouldn't have dreamed of missing it," I murmured, dropping my voice to the low, soothing tenor that Mama often required. "You know that."

I plucked a glass of champagne from a passing tray as she vanished into the crowd to go de-scent herself. I'd applied a thin layer of Om-Guard before I'd left the house, but I entirely expected my parents to hint that I should add another coat during the course of the evening. It was the family business, after all.

Legacy.

That word was heavy. I didn't want to be a legacy, I wanted to be an individual. I wanted to make choices for myself.

But I'd also lived a life of unimaginable privilege—one which that *legacy* had afforded me. It was suffocating, and yet, as far as problems went, life could have certainly dealt me a worse hand.

"Inika." Samira, an elderly member of the board who'd been serving as long as I'd lived, leaned in to give me an air kiss. "So wonderful to see you. That colour is stunning on you. Did you come alone tonight?"

I should have known the compliment wasn't free.

"I did." I smiled sweetly, deflecting the disapproval radiating from her pursed lips and the tight lines around her narrowed eyes.

"My grandson, Emmett, recently took a mate, did you hear?"

"I hadn't heard, no. That's wonderful. Please pass on my congratulations."

She hummed lightly, dissatisfied with my answer. Samira wasn't the only board member who'd hoped I'd pick a mate from their multitude of relatives. A suitable, well-connected alpha to take over the running of Om-Guard once my father stood down, leaving me safely tucked up in some country estate somewhere with as many children as my robust omega uterus could carry.

I was a great disappointment to all of them. Unfortunately for them, I was at least partially fuelled by spite, so that fact brought me great joy.

"You're very brave attending these things on your own." Samira sniffed, all alpha superiority. I had to give her credit, she was determined to keep pushing me for a reaction even though I was very intentionally not giving her one. "Not many unmated omegas would walk into a room like this without any sign of distress. It's an unnatural situation for you to be in."

"Is it?" I took a sip of my champagne. "I've never known any different."

I'd been attending these soirées since I was fresh out of the womb. Likely while I was still *in* the womb, though I wouldn't be shocked to hear that Mama had put herself under total house arrest the moment she started showing.

"No, I suppose not," Samira agreed, looking away to survey the room with barely contained disdain. "You're not a regular omega."

I was, though. At my core, I was a regular omega who wanted regular omega things. The things that made me *irregular* were pushed on me by the circumstances of my birth. By society. By my family. By everyone and everything, except myself.

Why was I so maudlin today? It must be because my heat was looming on the horizon again. It forced me to evaluate my life choices on an annual basis, and I wasn't always pleased with what I found.

"We should probably take our seats," I suggested, spotting Samira's mate across the room and exhaling slightly. We definitely weren't going to be sitting at the same table, at least.

Mama was already at the table when I arrived and took my seat between her and my uncle. Our group was mostly comprised of family, which meant I didn't need to answer any awkward questions, at least. By the time I'd finished university—still unmated, still failing to fulfil the only real duty that was expected of me—they'd stopped asking out of sheer embarrassment.

Papa was the last to appear, laughing and patting everyone on the back as he made his way through the room, his bald head shining in the chandelier light. He was always the most jovial person in the room, always ready with a funny quip and a charming compliment.

Papa had just enough memories of his life prior to immense wealth that he seemed able to relate to anyone. It was a skill that I actively worked to cultivate, and I'd always envied how it came to him so easily.

"Family!" he said cheerfully, standing behind his chair and opening his arms, surveying us grandly. "You're all here! I'm so glad you made it. Inika, my sweet girl, you look beautiful."

Papa was already on to his next compliment, singing my uncle's praises as he took his seat without giving me a chance to respond. Perhaps that was why Papa seemed to get along with everyone. He wasn't actually *conversing* with them, just *interacting* with them.

"You still working at Om-Guard?" Uncle Devyan asked gruffly, eyeing me warily. He had three big, boisterous alpha sons, and never seemed entirely sure how he was supposed to talk to me.

"Yes, Uncle. For the past twelve years."

He grunted, pouring himself a top-up from the bottles of wine on the table. Great chat.

Fortunately, the lights dimmed, and the presenters came on stage to begin the awards portion of the evening not long after. Papa knew everyone and happily supplied the table with factoids and anecdotes about all of them as the night progressed.

"This is us," Papa whispered loudly, leaning forwards and giving us all a cheerful, conspiratorial grin before sitting up at attention and focusing on the stage. I couldn't help but smile at his antics. Papa's energy was so jubilant at all times, it was difficult to not to feel a little of that joy seeping in. Often, I'd wondered if it was why Mama had been drawn to him in the first place. She had a nervous temperament and hated the social events that being mating to a Dara necessitated. But she wasn't nearly as stressed about any of that when Papa was around.

I tuned back in right as the presenter announced that the award for best employer would go to Om-Guard, pasting on my most brilliant smile right before the videographer panned over to me.

Papa and the Om-Guard management team made their way on stage as the hundreds of people in the room clapped and cheered. I stood up with the rest of the family, applauding right along with them, my cheeks hurting from smiling.

For all the pressure my position in life put on me, I couldn't deny how proud I was of my father and everything he'd accomplished. And I knew I'd never live up to it. There was no world in which I'd be standing on that stage, accepting an award for my entrepreneurial accomplishments.

Mama looked over at me, eyes shining with happy tears. She'd always been a crier.

"Oh, Inika. Isn't this wonderful?" She grabbed my hand, squeezing it tightly. "What an incredible life we have."

"Incredible," I agreed, my smile fixed in place.

Perhaps, someday, it would feel like that life belonged to me.

BLAKE

I scoffed quietly to myself as I approached the immaculately kept brick manor in Mayfair. Of course, the spoiled pretty princess omega whose staff had been nagging and demanding my services for months lived *here*. Where else?

I'd done my fair share of projects for wealthy wankers over the years, but they were my least favourite jobs to work on, even if the buildings themselves were incredible. Most of those clients didn't *actually* care about preserving the character and heritage of the home. They cared that I was booked out months in advance, and I'd worked on other rich fuckers' houses, and there'd been a bullshit article about me in the paper, stood in front of some freshly restored cornices like a tosser.

I should have been working on a beautiful chapel right now in collaboration with the historical society. But they ran out of money and put the project on hold, so here I was.

A staff member—an inoffensive-smelling beta with a faintly disdainful expression—opened the front door, pursing his lips at the sight of me. I didn't dress to impress clients; I dressed to *work*. If that offended Miss Uptown Omega, then maybe she'd pull the plug on this idea and send me on my way. She'd been first up on the cancellation waitlist, but I had other options.

"Blake Alwis?" the snobby butler asked, his nose wrinkling slightly in distaste at my affirmative nod. "Right this way, Ms Dara is expecting you."

Though, it would be slightly disappointing if the omega pulled the pin now, if only because I wanted to get a peek under the curtains at this magnificent property. It was undoubtedly a masterclass in craftsmanship.

The room that the butler led me to was the closest to the front door, limiting my opportunities to look around. Though, what I *could* see wasn't particularly worth looking at. It could be the interior of any modern build from this angle.

I added it to my list of crimes the wealthy had committed. They had plenty of money—just build a new house if you wanted it to look like a new house. Leave the ones with character for the rest of us.

Though the rest of us couldn't afford to live in Mayfair.

"Ms Dara? Mr Alwis is here to see you," the butler called through the door, announcing his presence with a gentle knock.

"Let him in."

My dislike for this wealthy pest of an omega who'd been hounding me continued to foment as the beta opened the study door, gesturing for me to enter. At what level of wealth did people stop opening their own doors? Did she even know how door handles worked or was that a poor person life skill?

"Mr Alwis. A pleasure to finally meet you."

I grunted in acknowledgement, sizing up the room as I stood in the doorway of the circular office. The curved bookshelves alone that lined the walls would have probably taken a significant chunk off my mortgage, and the black marble and oak desk in the centre of the room was clearly a custom piece, curved to fit the exact contours of the room. It suited the space, but I wasn't sure it suited the omega standing behind it.

Inika Dara was sleek and polished and expensive, to be sure. But she wasn't cold like I'd expected her to be. After just a few seconds of looking at her, it was clear that everything about her radiated warmth beneath that elegant, poised exterior.

Odd.

And, of course, she was fucking beautiful. Just my luck. Inika Dara had deep brown skin; thick wavy black hair, pulled into a low ponytail, and the darkest eyes I'd ever seen, framed by impossibly long eyelashes. Everything about her—from the high cheekbones to the plush lips, and her graceful neck screamed *elegance*.

Was she just born *looking* like that? Or was that a by-product of unimaginable wealth, too?

I hazarded a guess that Inika Dara was unmated too, though her lack of scent made it difficult to tell. She'd obviously slathered herself in scentshield lotion, which I grudgingly appreciated.

The silence had dragged on, but Ms Dara didn't seem to be in a rush to break it. She raised an eyebrow as she sized me up right back, probably unimpressed by me wearing jeans and a thick, well-worn sweater to meet a client. In stark contrast, she was dressed head-to-toe in black office wear—a high-necked tight sweater and fitted slacks.

Wasn't she an unemployed heiress? Perhaps I needed to revise my ideas about what unemployed heiresses looked like.

"Would you like to sit down, Mr Alwis?" Ms Dara asked, gesturing at the seat in front of the desk. "Or you could continue to loom in the doorway, if that's more comfortable."

I snorted, taken aback at her boldness. Then again, she'd probably gone through life saying whatever she wanted without consequences.

"Alternatively, we could move to the courtyard if you're concerned about my scent?" Ms Dara suggested.

I shook my head, trudging over to the desk and taking a seat as she delicately sat down in hers.

"I can't smell you," I muttered, slightly shocked that she'd raised the topic so easily. It wasn't the kind of thing well-bred omegas discussed, from my vague recollections of the public school my brother and I had been forced to attend.

"Excellent. Well, let's get to it, shall we? As you're probably aware from mine and my assistant's many emails..." She paused, giving me a long look. I supposed that this was probably the part where I should apologise for making her chase me down, but I wasn't so inclined. I didn't *want* to work for rich fucks who didn't appreciate the character of these old buildings anyway.

Her eyes almost seemed to flash with amusement for a moment, but then it was gone and she resumed speaking. "I'm looking to recreate a specific piece of plasterwork over a staircase and landing that was walled off for many years. Unfortunately, it's been long since removed, but I have the original plans for the house—well, the stables, as they were—and I've heard you're the very best at these kinds of projects. I'm told you use traditional materials like cow hair where needed to match original work, is that true?"

"It is," I replied gruffly, reluctantly impressed that she'd done her research, and was hiring based on more than the fact that I was busy and had inadvertently cultivated an air of exclusivity that seemed to appeal to the wealthy.

"Does it feel like you're part of a long-standing tradition, keeping those traditional methods alive?" she asked, tilting her head to the side as though she genuinely wanted to hear the answer to that question.

"I guess," I admitted gruffly. Nothing about this interaction was going the way I'd envisioned it.

She gave me a long look, the corners of her mouth twitching before she opened a drawer, pulling out a manila folder and sliding it across to me. "I made a copy of the plans for you to take a look at—you can keep those. Shall we go upstairs to see the space?"

I grunted in agreement, eyeing her slightly warily as we both stood. On reflection, it was weird that we'd had this meeting with no one else in the room, let alone going upstairs with her to where I presumed the more personal areas of the house were.

Sure, *regular* omegas went about their lives and got things done without a bodyguard following them everywhere, but I fully expected Inika Dara to have one. An entire squad, in fact.

Though, perhaps, what I actually expected her to have was a *mate*. How had an omega as coveted as the Om-Guard heiress not been mated off during her first heat?

We made our way out of her office, past a mostly glass wall that looked into a central courtyard, heading up a flight of stairs.

Honestly, all the money in the world couldn't buy good taste.

Converting an 1800s stables into a grand home would have undoubtedly required a lot of work, but it was unfortunate that whoever had done it hadn't left a trace of its original character on the inside. The walls were covered in tastefully expensive off-white luxury wallpaper, the many fireplaces I could see through open doors were stainless-steel edged gas inserts halfway up the walls, and the entire place was done up in shades of cream, beige, and brown.

It was a fucking travesty.

There wasn't a trace of raw brick or aged timber as Ms Dara led me upstairs. No reclaimed doors. Even the beautiful wooden window frames had been covered in a smooth layer of inoffensive eggshell paint.

"It's not very authentic, I know," Ms Dara said with a wry smile. Perhaps the look on my face had been projecting my thoughts. "It looked like this when I moved in—I wouldn't have chosen to remove so many of the original features."

"You didn't see anything you liked better when you were house hunting?" It wasn't like there was a shortage of obscenely expensive historical homes in this part of town.

Ms Dara's smile tightened a fraction before she fixed her perfectly pleasant expression back in place. "I didn't choose it. But I have no complaints. Obviously. It's a lovely home. I'm very grateful to live here."

I wasn't sure who she was trying to convince with that statement. She showed me to the space before quietly excusing herself to take a call. The butler with the judgemental hawk eyes reappeared to stare at me while I measured and photographed the area. He did it under the guise of polishing a side table, but he seemed oddly invested in shining one spot.

Ignoring his disapproving gasp, I knocked on the door to Ms Dara's office on my way out, poking my head in when she called for me to open it.

That ought to give the butler a conniption.

"I'm done here. If you're happy to proceed, then I'll be back in a couple of days to rip out the more recent plasterwork and get the space ready. It'd be helpful to have the surrounding hallway area cleared of furniture before then."

"That won't be a problem. I'll have Graeme see to it immediately."

Of course she would.

I grunted out some kind of acknowledgement before making for the front door. For some reason, everything about this project felt like it was going to be a challenge, which made absolutely no sense considering how incredibly basic it was. The area was small, and I was recreating an arched lath and plaster ceiling directly from the original plans, which required a lot less brainpower than reimagining it from scratch.

It must have been *her*.

Something about Inika Dara spelled trouble for me, and I had no interest in delving deeper to discover what that was.

I had the distinct feeling I might not like what I found.

I steeled myself to walk in the front door when I got home, already feeling the vibrating tension of alpha aggression radiating from inside the house.

We shouldn't live together.

Objectively, three grown alphas living under the same roof was a bad idea—we were territorial by nature, and our instincts demanded we push out any competition for resources.

But even if we'd all been cool-headed betas, it would have been a bad idea because we drove each other insane.

The first thing I heard when I opened the front door was Freya's sweet little voice of reason, and it broke my fucking heart. She was five. It wasn't her responsibility to mediate between full-grown adults.

"Everyone, just take a breath. Daddy, take a breath. See? Like this."

This wasn't her job. We were failing her.

"What's the problem now?" I grumbled, stomping into the kitchen.

Freya turned her exasperated gaze on me, both hands on her hips just like my mother used to do when standing her ground against rowdy alphas. "No shoes in the house, Uncle Blake."

I grumbled out an apology, trudging back to the front door to remove my work boots. As the resident omega, Freya set the rules on that sort of thing, and I needed to be better at following them.

"Right. What are you fighting about, then?" I asked, re-entering the too-small kitchen in my socks.

"Grandad wants to go down to the pub with Lewis and Jasper tonight," Freya said, calm and logical, as she always was. Leo and I hadn't sounded like that at five. We had been little assholes who got sent home from school for swearing.

"Alright." I looked between the three of them, trying to figure out what the problem was. Dad was at the pub most nights, probably to get away from the house and the abundance of tension that filled it.

"But Dad wants him to babysit," Freya said exasperatedly, looking at me like I was the problem now.

"I see." I watched Leo closely as he suddenly seemed very interested in washing the breakfast dishes he'd had all day to do. "Somewhere you need to be, Leo?"

He shot me a glare over his shoulder, pressing his lips together. He'd never admit in front of Freya that he wanted to go and fight in the illegal underground ring where he made the bulk of his money nowadays. But she wasn't a dumb kid. She'd picked up on the fact that whenever he wanted Grandad to babysit, he appeared at breakfast the next morning looking like he'd been through a meat grinder.

"We've got that thing, remember?" Leo asked, still scowling at me.

"Nope, it seems to have slipped my mind. Remind me?"

He shoved the frying pan into the water a little harder than necessary, sloshing bubbles everywhere.

Leo was a great fighter. One of the best at *Leviathan,* and the crowd *loved* him because he wasn't afraid to put his body through the wringer to get a win. But he was also a nightmare, and the club owners had decreed that he wasn't allowed on the premises without me, because someone had to keep him under control.

"Invite Lewis and Jasper around here and order a curry or something. I'll pay you back for it," Leo muttered, glancing hopefully at Dad. How Leo was the favourite son, I would never know. Dad hadn't eaten curry once since Mum died—clearly Leo hadn't been paying attention.

"I can come to the pub, Grandad," Freya piped up. "I'll bring my colouring and sit nice and quietly."

I exhaled heavily, glaring at Leo, who had the good sense to look at least a little sheepish.

"No need for all that, Frey," Dad said, patting Freya on the head. "Lewis and Jasper can come round here and you can help me make toad in the hole. How does that sound?"

Freya beamed up at him. She was an easily pleased kid, really. She just wanted some attention.

"I'm going to go to my room and draw them both a picture."

"I'm sure they'll love that," Dad assured her as she skipped off, giving me a warning look on the way past, like I was going to be the problem here.

Dad exhaled heavily as Leo was drying his hands, and my brother immediately spun around to face him, his body language all confrontation.

"Got something to say?"

Before everything had fallen apart, Dad might have risen to Leo's goading—even though Leo had always been his favourite—but he never did now. Sometimes, I wondered if that was why Leo still did it.

"Make smart decisions," Dad sighed, shuffling out of the room. His back must have been giving him grief today. "Remember, you have more than just *you* to think about. I'm going to call the boys."

Leo turned his combative glare on me, and I rolled my eyes.

"Save it for the ring. A heads-up would have been appreciated, by the way. What if I had plans tonight?"

Leo frowned. "You never have plans."

"Yeah, well, I'm going to start going out more."

"Where?"

"None of your business."

He snorted. "You're full of shit."

Siblings were a fucking curse. Though, I'd probably like him a lot more if we didn't live under the same roof.

"Whatever. I'm going to wash up. I'll meet you down here later. You should go hang out with Freya for a bit. Do some drawing with her."

Leo side-eyed me for the suggestion, but followed me up the stairs and headed to Freya's room because he knew I was right. He wouldn't be any use to her tomorrow.

A couple of hours later, we headed into the back entrance of *Leviathan*, descending the dark staircase to the basement where the fights were held.

They changed the times of the fights each time to throw off the authorities, and this one was early enough to attract mostly the after-work crowd. It was definitely Leo's preferred audience. They had deep pockets and weren't as cautious with their bets as the regulars.

"You're getting a little old for this, aren't you?" I grumbled, following Leo. The thud of the bass upstairs was already giving me a headache, and the ever-present stickiness of the floor was more viscerally disgusting to me each year.

I wanted to be at home. On the couch. Ideally, with a cup of tea and some chocolate biscuits, and no people around me.

"No. I'll fight until I'm too old to climb into the ring."

"Or until you're too injured to do it anymore. Anything other than get a proper job, hm?"

Leo shook his head slightly, but he was in a good mood. This was his happy place. Nothing I said bothered him here. He saved all his ire for his opponents.

"There you are!" Ronnie yelled over the noise of the crowd. "Get over here, Leo!"

"Are you going to finally get back in the ring tonight?" Leo called over his shoulder.

I snorted, shaking my head. I hadn't fought in *years*. The money wasn't something to be sniffed at, and the radiator in Freya's room needed to be replaced. But I'd rather earn my money the old-fashioned way, and not ruin my professional reputation by showing up to work with a bust-up face.

I couldn't imagine what Inika Dara would think if I walked into her home looking the way Leo did after a fight. It would probably traumatise the little omega princess.

Leo disappeared into the crowd to talk to Ronnie, while I got myself a pint and found a good pillar to lean against.

A group of betas in tailored suits were clinking their glasses together nearby, laughing loudly. I wondered if they ran in the same circles as the Om-Guard heiress? No, surely not. Their suits looked nice, but not *that* nice.

Why the fuck was I thinking about her, anyway? I shook my head slightly, taking a sip of my beer. I didn't usually think about my clients at all once I left work for the day.

It was just because she was an unmated omega, that was all.

A beautiful unmated omega.

But that was the reason she was in my head. It wasn't as though I spent an abundance of time around unmated omegas. I never had. After finishing school, I'd immediately joined the army, and then I'd focused on building the business. By the time I'd even *considered* getting to know some omegas and settling down, Leo and Freya's lives imploded, followed shortly by Dad's, and everyone moved in with me.

An omega of my own wasn't in the cards for me anymore. I couldn't expect anyone else to put up with my fucked-up family, and bringing them into that situation would be cruel. Besides, Freya needed me. I didn't want to split my focus by having kids of my own.

I exhaled heavily into my beer, my fingers tightening slightly around the glass. That's what that weird feeling had been when I'd left Inika Dara's house.

Sexual attraction.

How very fucking inconvenient.

Chapter 3

INIKA

"That was brutal," Stasia whined, flopping forwards in the foyer of the Pilates studio post-workout to rub her thighs. "George is going to have to give me the *longest* massage tonight."

The three of us mumbled some vaguely supportive words of agreement, even though we all knew Stasia paid a professional for massages. It was probably judgemental of me to even think it, but George and Stasia didn't *look* like a couple who touched each other outside of heats. Frankly, none of my friends had touch-feely matings, but they were basically all but arranged, so I supposed that was to be expected.

Honestly, I didn't think Stasia could stand George most of the time, but they were mated now and what was done was done.

"Are you going to do a class tomorrow?" Brigitte asked while Stasia and Ivy went to the bar to collect our kale and turmeric smoothies. "Miranda is in Guernsey for the week—some work thing. I figure I may as well do one each day. I haven't got anything else going on."

"I can't tomorrow. My presence has been requested at an Om-Guard board meeting."

Brigitte raised an eyebrow at me. "I thought you were some kind of..." She flicked her hand dismissively. "You know, employee or something. Since when do you attend board meetings?"

"This will be the first," I admitted.

Brigitte was the most stoic of all of us—and it sometimes came across as aloof—but she was also the fiercest friend. "Well, that's good, isn't it? Your father finally recognises that you deserve a seat at the leadership table based entirely on your own merits instead of waiting for you to take a mate."

I gave her a strained smile. "I'm not quite so optimistic. The board likely just wants an opportunity to tell me for themselves that I need to hurry up and pick a man. They probably know that Papa is too gentle to push the issue."

I wouldn't be at all surprised if my cousin, Avi, was in attendance too, being the next alpha of kin of my generation. No one had ever outright stated that he was the backup option, but they didn't need to.

I'd insisted on going in at the ground floor and working my way up through Om-Guard, wanting to learn the ropes and add genuine value to the business. Avi had been appointed Marketing Director without a shred of experience in either marketing or directing. I pitied the team of betas who worked underneath him, tirelessly ignoring all of his stupid ideas while still making it seem like they were following his orders.

"There you ladies are," Spencer said, bowing with a flourish as he entered the studio before politely kissing Ivy on the cheek. "Ivy, I thought I'd lost you. We need to get on the road, darling."

She gave him a tight-lipped smile before handing me my smoothie, a look of far more genuine affection on her face. Spencer had always been a bit of a playboy, and Ivy was an assortment of insecurities hidden beneath the most beautiful exterior I'd ever seen. Ten years into their mating, and they seemed just as distant with each other now as they had been when they'd first emerged from her nest.

"How was class?" Spencer asked, surveying the group.

"Agony," Stasia replied dramatically, half paying attention to us, half focused on her phone. "Where are you two off to?"

"The lodge for the week," he replied, referring to his parents' hunting lodge in Somerset. "We're getting all the cousins together while they're off school, that sort of thing."

"Oh, are the boys in the car?" I asked, perking up. Their three sons were rambunctious—but delightful—little monsters, and we rarely got to see them.

"Oh no. The nanny has already taken them down," Ivy replied with a light laugh. "Frankly, I wouldn't survive a car ride with all three."

"How are you finding this nanny?" Stasia asked, setting Ivy off on a long tangent about her struggle to find anyone she liked, while Brigitte and I—both child-free—sipped our smoothies in silence.

"Inika!" Spencer said suddenly, slapping his thigh and making me startle. "I meant to tell you, Hugo is moving back from Copenhagen. His company has transferred him back to the London office. Should be here by the end of the month, if I recall correctly. You remember Hugo, right? He's an old school friend of mine."

I shook my head, having only the vaguest recollections of Spencer's boarding school friends from when he and Ivy first met.

"He's an Operations Director for some multinational—I forget the details, but it sounds very impressive, no? *Excellent* family too. Titled. His father is the Marquess of Hastings, and Hugo is the heir apparent."

"I see."

It was a good thing I'd practically bathed in Om-Guard after my workout. The others wouldn't smell the stress pheromones coming off me, at least.

Why did I even react this way? On paper, Hugo sounded like exactly the kind of alpha I should be entertaining. Of course, I hadn't liked any of those alphas in the past, but there was always the possibility that this one was both a decent human being, interesting enough to hold a conversation, and capable of fucking me properly.

None of them had been in the past, but maybe.

A brief image of Blake Alwis, the grumpy alpha plasterer, popped into my head unbidden, and I swallowed, my mouth suddenly dry. I'd had to shower, masturbate, then shower again after he'd left.

He had an abysmal personality, but I'd bet my entire fortune that Blake Alwis could *fuck*.

He was gorgeous too. Deep brown skin. Short black hair. *Thick* beard. Broad shoulders that looked like they'd make an excellent seat. He really ticked all of the boxes.

It was incredibly inappropriate for me to think of him that way, of course. But they were just harmless thoughts, right? He never had to know.

"Hugo was messing around with some Danish beta for years," Spencer continued, rudely yanking my wandering thoughts back into the present. "It's been a real source of stress for his family that he didn't have an omega. A proper mate, you know? Anyway, that's all done now. You two would get along swimmingly, don't you think, Ivy?"

Ivy nodded enthusiastically, giving me a wide-eyed look. Sometimes I wondered if she really wanted me to find an alpha to fall in love with or if it was more of a misery-loves-company situation. "Oh yes. Hugo is lovely. Your parents would adore him."

"A ringing endorsement," Brigitte murmured, though I knew deep down she'd also like to see me mated off, though I suspected for different reasons than the others. For someone who was so open-minded in other areas, Brigitte had a deep dislike for the very concept of Prendre and agencies like it, and hated that I used them for my heats. Until she'd been mated, she suffered through them alone, seeing it as a trial that all unmated omegas had to go through.

Unfortunately for her, I'd never found much glory in needless suffering.

"Why don't you set up something where they can meet?" Stasia suggested excitedly. "Oh, we haven't been for tapas in *forever*. Doesn't that sound wonderful, Inika? A titled, single alpha—at our age!"

I hummed in agreement without much enthusiasm. There was no use pointing out that I'd likely met him before, and there had clearly been no sparks then. For all their supportive words about how I shouldn't settle, I knew my friends all felt that at thirty-four the pickings were slim and I should just take what I could get.

If finding someone was all I cared about, I could have been mated a thousand times over by now. Alphas were not a scarcity. Alphas were in abundance.

I wanted love.

I wanted to fall in love with someone that I actually enjoyed spending time with. I wanted them to fuck me like they hated me, then hold me like they adored me.

Was that really too much to ask?

"Tapas sounds great. Let's make it happen when we're back from the lodge," Spencer said with a self-satisfied grin. I wondered if Hugo knew he was being set up—the poor bloke was probably still pining after the Danish beta, and his friends were already trying to pair him off on this side of the Channel. "We should probably get going, Ivy."

We all headed for the front doors and said our goodbyes, and I promised to meet Brigitte for a class later in the week as Lúcás pulled up to the curb to collect me.

"Where to today, Miss?" Lúcás asked, grinning at me cheerfully in the rearview mirror.

"I have a skin appointment at Étincelle."

"Étincelle it is," he called back, butchering the pronunciation slightly as he put the car in drive.

I slumped back in the leather seat, looking out the window at the grey, dreary day outside. Objectively, I had a wonderful life. A better life than *so* many people had. Most people, even. And yet, I couldn't help feeling like the walls were always a hairsbreadth away from closing in on me.

It was incredibly frustrating. Because if I couldn't be happy with *everything* that I had, then perhaps happiness just wasn't on the cards for me at all.

"They're ready for you now, Ms Dara," Brian said, poking his head around the door.

I stood up, smoothing down my business-appropriate navy slacks and heading into the boardroom. I'd arrived when I'd been told to arrive, and the meeting had been well and truly in progress by then. Whatever I was here for, it was merely as a featured guest.

"Welcome, welcome," Papa said, gesturing for me to take a seat at the round table between him and Samira. "Thank you for joining us, Inika."

"Thank you for having me," I murmured back, struggling to keep my spine straight with so much oppressive alpha energy in the room.

"Have you had a good day, my darling girl?" Papa asked, giving me an encouraging smile. I did my best to relax, discreetly taking a few calming breaths while I sat down and fussed a little in my seat.

He was reacting to my nervous energy, his alpha instincts telling him to soothe an omega under his protection. As if I wasn't struggling enough to look like a professional.

"Fine. Thank you, Papa."

"I'm sure you know why you're here?" Olivier, one of the other board members, asked from across the table.

I suspected that I did, but I wasn't about to make their lives easier by telling them that.

"I'm afraid not."

"Ah." Olivier shifted uncomfortably in his seat. "We'd, uh, like you to be part of the succession planning discussion."

"Oh?" I folded my hands in my lap and made a show of waiting patiently for them to continue, at which everyone appeared to get uncomfortable and fall silent again.

It was outrageous that alphas were credited with being the bravest of the three designations. In battle, perhaps. But when faced with the possibility of even a vaguely uncomfortable conversation, there wasn't a shred of courage to be found.

"Inika," Samira began gently. Condescendingly. "I'm sure we don't need to point out to you that no International-100 company is led by an unmated omega. It's never been done before. It's a big responsibility, and omegas already have so many responsibilities. Other strengths. Impressive strengths! Things that alphas can't do."

The fact that they all made such a show of loudly agreeing annoyed me even more than their cowardly silence.

"Unless I had a mate to help me," I supplied flatly.

The alphas all seemed to relax at the realisation that they wouldn't have to bring it up first.

"Well, yes. Exactly," Samira agreed, nodding her head enthusiastically.

I looked at Papa, trying to get an idea of just how far he would push this idea, but he was diligently looking everywhere except at me. I didn't like to think ill of the man who had done so much for me, but I couldn't help finding his actions in that moment to be a little spineless.

Would it really have been so difficult to offer me a little reassurance? To let the board know he had no intention of pushing me beyond my comfort levels, as he'd always promised me in private?

Perhaps he didn't feel that way in public.

"So, is any random alpha I pick off the street better suited to lead Om-Guard than me? Or is there a shortlist you'd like me to choose from?" I asked mildly, revelling in their discomfited looks. As if anyone here had the right to be more uncomfortable than me, and I wasn't making a production out of it.

"Of course not." Papa laughed nervously. "We would never expect you to make such a big decision like who you bond yourself to based on managerial skills." There was another uncomfortable smattering of laughter. "It's more that when you choose a mate, we will need to meet with him and talk to him... Figure out what his involvement—and therefore your involvement—will look like. Everything can be learned, of course."

"Absolutely," Samira agreed. "Temperament is a key consideration. And a general... suitability. For this lifestyle. It's not everyone, you know."

They weren't giving me a shortlist of names, but they may as well have. It was clear that they wanted a particular sort of alpha.

They'd take Hugo in a heartbeat, though none of us had even met the guy yet. Based on Spencer's words, he perfectly fit the mould.

Hans, one of the Board members who'd held a grudge against me for a decade now because I hadn't mated his son, cleared his throat. "Inika, we understand that this is a big commitment for you. However, we have been putting off decisions around succession planning for years now, and frankly, we can't do it any longer. We will be finalising it by the end of the financial year, come what may."

I could only take a mate during my annual heat, so I heard the deadline in Hans's edict, despite him leaving it unsaid.

Emerge from your nest after your next heat—in a month—mated to a suitably posh alpha who can have all the grown-up thoughts that your soft, little omega brain can't handle, or get out of the way.

"This isn't a decision we have taken lightly, Inika," Papa said hurriedly, giving me another shaky smile. "We know how hard you've worked for Om-Guard all these years. And regardless of what happens, you will always be my daughter, and you will always be taken care of—"

"Thank you, Papa." My ego could only take so much of a beating.

The awkward silence at the table was deafening, and my instincts were clawing at my insides, demanding that I soothe and appease, and do everything in my power to make the alphas feel better.

I had to get out of here before I absolutely debased myself and gave them even more reasons to write me off as an unstable omega.

"Was there anything else you wanted to discuss with me?" I asked through gritted teeth.

If my smile was forced, it was nothing on Papa's. He looked almost pained. He hated having hard conversations. In his mind, life should never be anything other than comfortable and filled with joy.

"That's the only thing on the agenda for you," Brian replied tightly, his beta nervous system probably as overwhelmed as mine by the heightened alpha energy in the room.

"Wonderful. I won't hold you up then."

Just standing up took effort. My legs trembled under the oppressive weight of dissatisfaction in the room. If I'd let my instincts rule me, I'd have crawled under the table and curled up in the fetal position, desperately wishing for the comfort of my nest.

However, I was no fledgling omega. I'd made it this far in life with my dignity intact, and I wasn't going to ruin it now.

I pushed myself to make eye contact and managed a mostly serene smile as Brian escorted me out of the room, not exhaling until I was in the lift alone, slumped against the railing that dug uncomfortably into my ribs.

I'd done everything I could. I'd graduated with a first. I'd got my MBA. I'd invested my inheritance from my grandparents wisely, impressing Papa with my good business acumen. I'd worked in the Om-Guard product planning department for years, and shocked every manager I'd ever had with my work ethic and the valuable contributions I'd made to the team.

If I'd been an alpha, it would have been enough. *More* than enough. Spoiled little trust fund babies I'd known my whole life inherited their family businesses all the time, and they'd worked half as hard and had a quarter of the common sense that I had.

It was, to put it bluntly, a fucking joke.

Pull yourself together, Inika. You weren't even sure that you wanted *Om-Guard.*

I was self-aware enough that sulking about not inheriting a giant corporation made me feel slightly ill—it wasn't as though I *deserved* Om-Guard. And it had always been something planned *for* me rather than something I'd chosen for myself.

But if I was an alpha, it would have been mine, no questions asked.

Chapter 4

BLAKE

"Hey." I banged on Leo's door first thing in the morning, not bothering to be gentle about it. "I'm coming in."

He groaned, yanking the blanket over his head and rolling towards the wall as I opened the door.

"It stinks in here," I muttered, picking over the piles of laundry on the floor to pull open the curtains and throw open the window. Once upon a time, when I'd lived here alone, this room had been my office space. Leo had thoroughly ruined it with his stench now, and I mostly worked from the dining table when I remembered to do invoicing. "Come to work with me today."

"Fuck off," Leo mumbled, his voice muffled by his pillow.

"What's your excuse this time? You won the fight. You can work with a few bruises."

"Don't be a dick. You know it's more than a few bruises. I'm not getting out of bed."

The scaffolding had gone up, and the Dara project required minimal demolition, at least. When Inika—*Ms Dara,* I reminded myself—had the building team through to open up a covered-up staircase, they'd left the space nice and tidy. The only thing that had to come out was the false ceiling—complete with eighties-era plasterwork—that was hiding the cavity above where the arches would have once been.

I wasn't opposed to manual labour—far from it—but this was a task that Leo could easily help me with. Instead, he was laid up in bed, in the house that I paid for, while Dad and I had got Freya ready for school.

"This is ridiculous, Leo," I sighed. "You're no bloody help to anyone like this."

All I got in response was a grunting snore.

This wasn't how it was meant to be. When we'd finished our decade in the army, Leo and I had sworn we were going to make something of ourselves. Run our own business. Start families of our own. Take care of our parents in their old age. We'd managed half of everything, I supposed. It didn't feel particularly rewarding.

I slammed the door behind me, hoping it would wake him up again, before heading downstairs to shove my boots on and head out. Fortunately, Dad was already walking Freya to school, so neither of them were around to witness my bad mood or Leo's bullshit.

Not that they hadn't seen it before, but they deserved better. Dad was meant to be having a relaxing retirement. Freya was meant to be enjoying her childhood. They didn't need this shit.

By the time I'd ripped out the old ceiling at the Dara house, I was in a foul mood, but at least I'd been mostly left to my own devices by both the client and her retinue of staff. This staircase I was working over really only led to one room, and even that was accessible by going up the main stairs and through the corridors that formed a rectangle around the central courtyard. I imagined that the main reason for reopening it was to bring in natural light from the surrounding windows, rather than for any practical purpose as a pathway.

I cleaned up as best I could—loading the van up with rubbish to dispose of—and washed some of the dust off myself in the small, sleek bathroom down the hall. The one section of lath-and-plaster decorative arches was definitely going to stand out in a house of clean lines and LED pendant lights. But I was no interior decorator. I just did what I was paid to do.

By the time I emerged, it was to find a perfectly put-together omega standing on the dust-covered plastic sheet that protected the floor, peering up at the ceiling through the scaffolds.

"That already looks so much better."

I grunted in agreement, because it *did* look better. The original arched laths were in pretty good condition, though some would need replacing. If nothing else, the small space felt immediately grander and more interesting with the low false ceiling removed.

The contrast of Inika's expensive outfit and the dusty, plain surroundings and paint-splattered scaffolding was a jarring one. It was her house, but she didn't belong *here*. Not amongst all this filth.

"Is this going to be a regular occurrence?"

Inika tipped her chin up stubbornly, and I barely swallowed down an alpha growl of disapproval. Disapproval, and a little something more that I didn't want to acknowledge.

I should have jerked off this morning. Being in the presence of an unmated omega—a beautiful, confident, elegant omega, no less—was playing havoc with my libido. When was the last time I'd got laid? I couldn't even remember. I was too fucking tired to put in enough effort to make that happen.

"You mean, am I regularly going to be looking at the progress *in my own house?*" she asked mildly, her shiny black heels already covered in a thin sheen of dust.

"It was just a question."

"It was a ludicrous question." She planted her hands on her hips, surveying the space with a critical eye as if she had any idea what she was looking for.

Fuck. There was no reason for this to feel like foreplay, and yet...

I exhaled heavily. Clearly unmated alphas and omegas shouldn't be alone together. It was a recipe for disaster.

"You're getting dirt all over your fancy outfit."

Inika glanced down in surprise. It probably wasn't a fancy outfit to her, but the navy trousers and silky blouse looked posh to me.

"My meeting is over. I don't have to look nice anymore." She flicked her hand dismissively, probably because a member of staff would see that the outfit was dry cleaned and she'd never have to think about it again. "Did you wake up on the wrong side of the bed this morning?"

"No. I'm always this charming."

Inika let out a small laugh, and even that sounded expensive. "Could you walk me through what the next steps are in here?"

She truly was my least favourite kind of client.

"Repair what needs repairing. Plaster. Fancier plaster." If she wanted a contractor who'd hold her hand through the entire process, she should have hired someone else.

"Aren't you helpful?" Inika replied, rolling her eyes. The bratty gesture pushed me over the edge of professionalism and well and truly into alpha mode.

"Listen, princess, I'm busy. I've budgeted a set amount of hours to get this job done, and those hours don't include explaining what I'm doing to the client every step of the way."

Inika sucked in a breath, her eyes widening slightly. I hazarded that no one had ever spoken to her so plainly in her life, and she was probably going to crawl into her million-pound nest and cry about it for the rest of the afternoon.

How nice to be rich and unemployed enough for a workday breakdown in bed.

"You hired me because I'm the best," I continued. "So stay out of my way and let me do my job."

You're being an asshole, I told myself. I was sleep deprived from accompanying Leo to his fight, then Freya had woken up at three am after a bad dream. I'd been stuck working on my own all day because my brother was too useless to get out of bed, and that butler had definitely been spying on me from around the corner earlier.

"I can't believe you just spoke to me like that," Inika said in disbelief, though her voice had taken on a breathy quality that it hadn't had a moment ago.

And then I smelled it. The rich, syrupy scent of omega perfume. I inhaled deeply, not even trying to hide it.

Fuck.

She smelled so... off-limits.

A possessive growl rumbled up from my chest, my cock hardening so quickly, my head spun. Inika pressed her thighs together, her eyes hazy with desire. The air was thick with the scent of omega perfume and bad decisions.

"It smells like you're sick of alphas talking to you like you're made of glass if you're getting all hot and bothered over a few plain words, princess."

This is a highly inappropriate way to speak to a client, I attempted to remind myself.

"You might be right," Inika rasped, making me forget any and all warnings I'd been giving myself. "You're obscenely rude. I should hate it."

"But you don't."

"But I don't," she agreed breathlessly. The thin tether of self-control I'd been clinging onto snapped entirely.

"Does it make your pussy wet?"

Inika's face flamed at the crude question, but the scent of her slick only grew more potent as she nodded. What was I *doing*? I'd gone far beyond the point of unprofessionalism that could be easily brushed off.

"Give me words, princess."

"Yes. Yes, it makes my pussy wet."

Fuck.

She's your client, the angel on my shoulder reminded me.

Fuck her anyway, said the devil.

"You should leave," I growled, my cock aching in my suddenly uncomfortable work trousers.

"I don't want to leave."

I exhaled heavily, my burgeoning knot already throbbing.

"Then get on your knees, omega." It was phrased as an order, but there was no alpha command in my voice. Aside from not wanting to get arrested for unlawfully using my bark on an omega I had no claim on, Inika held all the power here—even if it didn't look like it. The moment she wanted any of this to stop, it would stop.

Any minute now, she'd remember that we were in a hallway. That any of her staff could come across us. That I was who I was, and she was who she was.

Any minute now.

Inika dropped down on the plastic sheet with a light thud, white dust instantly coating her expensive-looking navy trousers.

I wanted to ruin her.

I wanted her begging and weeping around my knot. I wanted to see that perfect make-up smeared and messy, mascara running down her cheeks. I wanted her slick coating my skin.

It was the most primal, feral desire I'd ever experienced in my life.

"Are you going to fuck me?" she asked. The blunt question delivered in her crisp, posh accent made my knot ache.

"You haven't earned my cock yet." I took a step towards her, the potent scent of her slick drawing me in. "Undo your trousers."

Inika held my gaze as she complied, tugging down the zip and revealing a hint of silky black fabric underneath.

I was walking a dangerous line here—one that I shouldn't have been walking without a proper conversation first—based purely on Inika saying she liked how rude I was. Desires that I rarely got to indulge in rose sharply to the surface.

"What's your safe word?" I asked gruffly, battling the alpha instinct to tell her to bend over and present her pussy for me.

"Audit."

"Audit," I repeated firmly. "You say it and everything stops. Pull your knickers aside. Touch yourself. I want to see that slick seeping through your trousers."

Inika shuddered, doing what I asked. I couldn't see anything beyond her hand moving, but I didn't need to. The moment was plenty erotic enough, and I was trying to maintain some semblance of restraint. We didn't have the luxury of getting carried away—not when someone could come across us at any moment.

"Look at you," I murmured, savouring the sound of her fingers playing with her wet pussy. "Absolutely filthy. Do you do this for all your contractors, hm? Kneel down in the dust with your cunt out?"

"No," she rasped. "Just you."

"You would say that, though. Wouldn't you?" I tutted in disapproval. "And here was me thinking you were such a classy omega."

"I am," Inika whined, her hand moving faster now.

"Are you? I'm not making you fuck your fingers on the ground for me, Inika. There was no alpha command in my voice. I told you that you should leave."

"I chose this," Inika insisted breathily, justifying herself. It would be just my luck that she was perfect at this. "I want this."

I hummed in agreement. "Tell me why that is, princess."

She was getting close now. I could feel it. I grabbed my cock through my trousers, giving it a rough squeeze. How I was going to function after this was a mystery I had yet to solve.

Though, there was always the chance that Inika would fire me right after she orgasmed. At least then I could go home and fuck my hand for a few hours.

"Answer me, omega," I pressed, wanting her to say it. Wanting her to sink to the level of depravity that I was already wallowing in.

"I'm usually good. So good."

"But right now?"

"I don't feel like a good girl."

"You don't look like one either, kneeling in the dust with your pussy out. What do you look like?"

"I look like a slut," Inika rasped, her voice cracking on a breathy moan as she found her release. A shudder ran down my spine.

"That's right," I soothed, closing the distance between us but not touching her. She was eye-level with the outline of my hard cock in my jeans, her gaze hazy as she stared at it. "You do. A beautiful, perfect, needy little slut. Isn't that right?"

Inika nodded, dragging her eyes up to my face. Considering the submissive position she was in and the fact that our alpha-omega instincts were entirely in the driver's seat, it was impressive that she maintained such steady eye contact.

"Get up, princess. Let me taste those fingers."

Inika climbed up on shaky legs, her dust-covered trousers still unbuttoned. Her lips were parted as she raised her fingers to mine, and I grasped her wrist, pulling her in to close the distance, and groaning aloud at the first taste of her slick on my tongue.

Absolutely fucking *decadent*. I wanted nothing more than to rip her clothes off and get a taste directly from the source. But we'd pushed our luck already. I'd opened the hallway windows for the dust, but we'd need a lot more than a faint breeze to carry away the scent of omega slick.

Reluctantly, I pulled away, dropping my hands to zip up her trousers, my knuckles brushing at the soaked fabric of her knickers in the process.

"You're not going to fuck me?" Inika asked, sounding gratifyingly disappointed.

My dick was so heavy, it was going to be a challenging walk just to get back to the van.

"Sleep on that idea, princess. Let me know what you think of it tomorrow."

She'd either take me up on it, or fire me. Either way, it was probably best that she gave the idea some thought first. I didn't want her having regrets.

To be completely honest, Inika Dara was a wealthy omega from a powerful family, and she absolutely had the ability to ruin my life. Getting involved with her at all was foolish on my part, but apparently my dick was in the driver's seat and wouldn't be convinced otherwise.

Inika nodded, looking suddenly sheepish. "I don't usually... you know. That was very out of character for me."

"Likewise," I assured her. "I've never crossed that line with a client before."

"I'm guessing most of your clients aren't unmated omegas," Inika said wryly.

"No, they're not."

Some of the tension eased from my shoulders that at least we were on the same page. That was all this was. An unmated alpha and an unmated omega with surprisingly compatible kinks getting carried away in the heat of the moment. It happened. We were horny beings by nature. It didn't *have* to be a disaster.

"Message me tomorrow," I reiterated, taking a step back. "When you've had time to think. Until then, Inika."

"Until then, Blake," she repeated faintly.

The lingering scent of her perfume haunted me the entire drive home.

Chapter 5

INIKA

I woke up panting, my silk pyjama shorts sticking to my thighs with slick, and groaned as I threw off the assortment of bedding that made up my nest.

My heat was a few weeks away, but that was in no way to blame for my current situation.

No. The current mess between my thighs was pure Blake.

I'd had plenty of incredible sexual encounters in my time. Actual sex even, not just masturbating in a dusty hallway. And yet, this was the first time I'd ever woken up in my nest so horny I was about to die just *dreaming* about it.

Sleep on that idea, princess.

Blake had made it sound like the ball was completely in my court as to whether we did anything further—which was very respectful of him—but what if *he'd* changed *his* mind? Blake may have enjoyed himself in the heat of the moment, but there was a real possibility that he'd filed a complaint about my irresponsible use of omega perfume the moment his sexual haze had worn off.

I was going to be highly annoyed with myself if I'd scared off one of the most in-demand tradesmen in London because my vagina was incapable of behaving in his presence. Especially if I scared him off before I even got to sleep with him. I suspected he would provide a plethora of memories that would get me through any lonely nights in my nest.

Sleep on that idea, princess.

The decision was simple on my part, but I was oddly unconfident that he would feel the same way. It was an uncertainty that I was unaccustomed to experiencing.

I was no breathtaking beauty in the grand scheme of things, but alphas usually lined up for me anyway. And why wouldn't they? Mating me would materially change their lives. Rejection was not an obstacle I had particularly encountered in my romantic life.

The sheets tangled in my legs as I wriggled up the bed, fumbling around on the bedside table for my phone. Clutching it close, I burrowed back into my blankets, pulling them over my head until I was properly surrounded by the comfort of my nest again.

Inika: I've slept on it.

I startled as my phone lit up almost instantly in response. Had he been waiting for my message? Blake didn't strike me as the type to be glued to his device.

Blake: And?

My stomach fluttered. The way he spoke to me was *so* curt. And yet he seemed intently interested in me, and it was the contrast between the two, the fine line he was straddling, that seemed to do it for me.

Or perhaps it was just the novelty of it all?

I probably shouldn't examine it too closely, or I'd talk myself out of a good time.

Inika: The desires I expressed yesterday haven't changed.

Was that too formal? Blake probably thought I was some posh robot, but I didn't know how to be flirty in writing.

Blake: Use your words, princess.

I fought my way back out of the blankets, feeling around in the drawer next to the bed until I found my favourite toy.

I'd produced so much slick from my dreams that the fake cock slid in with no resistance, the buzz of the vibrator muffled as I clamped it between my thighs to hold it in place so I could reply.

Like a lady.

Inika: I want you to fuck me.

Before I could panic about the boldness of that message, he'd already replied.

Blake: Of course you do. But I have work to do. Ask me nicely at 3 o'clock.

That arrogant prick. That arrogant, sexy, *outrageous* prick.

I set the phone aside and rolled onto my front so I could fuck myself with my toy at a better angle, rocking my hips back until the fat silicone knot was wedged at my entrance. I'd never got the hang of fully taking a fake knot—which was a large part of the reason I used an agency for my heats—but I still managed several quality orgasms before I crawled out of my nest, making the sprint of shame to the en suite before I trailed slick everywhere.

By the time I emerged—in a far shorter, flirtier skirt than I usually wore to work from home—I could hear Blake hammering away in the stairwell. I was tempted to have a peek, but I suspected that if I distracted him before three o'clock, Blake might send me back to my nest with only my silicone knot for comfort.

Blake Alwis was a man of words from his head to his toes, that much was obvious about him.

"Your breakfast, Ms Dara," Graeme said, quietly letting himself into my office with a tray of coffee, fruit, and yoghurt as I logged on to my computer.

"Thank you, Graeme."

He hovered after he set the tray down, his usual way of letting me know that he had something he wanted to say despite how many times I'd told him that he should feel free to speak his mind.

The hovering made my eye twitch.

"Is everything okay, Graeme?"

Graeme cleared his throat. "This contractor of yours..."

"Ah." I'd put the ventilation system on the maximum post-sex setting yesterday, which should have been enough to hide my tracks, considering all of my staff were betas and their noses weren't so sensitive. Then again, Graeme had worked around alphas and omegas for decades and was perhaps more attuned to it. "Mr Alwis. What about him?"

He winced at my bluntness. Graeme had worked for my parents for years before coming with me to my household, and if I could make the choice again, I'd have insisted he stay with them. My mother was the kind of omega he enjoyed dealing with—quiet, soothing, obedient. She'd never been difficult a day in her life.

"You're, er, quite certain he's the best for the job?"

"Quite certain. He comes highly recommended. Do you have concerns about his workmanship?" I asked, tilting my head to the side in faux confusion.

"No, no. His work seems... perfectly acceptable." I let the silence linger, encouraging him to get to the point. It was a skill that had taken some honing, and I still struggled with it. Omegas soothed and flattered. They didn't allow any awkwardness to settle in.

Graeme seemed to debate internally with himself before settling on an explanation. "Your father might have some reservations about having an unmated alpha in the house."

"Perhaps he would, but this is not my father's house." Graeme's cheeks pinkened, and I took pity on him. "Thank you for your concern, Graeme. I appreciate that you have my best interests at heart."

I kept my voice calm and even, but left no room for argument. Graeme nodded tersely, already excusing himself from the office. Undoubtedly, he would raise his concerns with my parents, and I would receive an anxious call from Mama later today, begging for me to stay with them.

There was some comfort in the predictability, I supposed.

It was a dull morning of emails and video calls, followed by a dull afternoon working on a report I was compiling on scent-neutralising SPF. While it wasn't particularly interesting to write, I had high hopes for how it would be received. Sun cream aligned nicely with our brand and Om-Guard's existing product range, while giving us room to expand into new areas.

Product research wasn't my dream job by any stretch of the imagination, but seeing the tangible results of my work ending up on shop shelves was somewhat rewarding. And that was all I really wanted, in the end. To make an impact in some small way, to *do* something, rather than just floating through life, barely touching the sides.

Incoming video call: Mama

I slumped for a moment before straightening my posture and accepting the call, setting my phone on the magnetic mount so I had a good angle.

"Oh, there you are, Inika." Mama was already wringing her hands, her phone sat on the coffee table in the drawing room, angled up under her chin. "I just spoke to Graeme. I was so worried you wouldn't answer the phone, Inie."

I wouldn't have answered if you'd called after three.

"Graeme says there is an *unmated alpha* in your house," she added in a scandalised whisper.

"Mama, I'm completely fine. Graeme is worrying over nothing."

"An unmated alpha, Inika!" she whisper-shouted, peering down at the camera with wide eyes. "Even if he is a nice, respectful man—Graeme offered me no reassurance on this front—it isn't a good look, Inie, for you to stay there alone."

"I'm never alone. I have an entire retinue of staff, Mama."

"Why would you even want to stay in the house while it's having work done? The dust!" She tutted impatiently. "Nonsense. Come stay here, Inie. You know Papa and I would love to have you."

"I'm fine here, Mama."

"Or go on holiday! We can go together. How long will these repairs take? Let's spend a few days shopping in Paris. Or perhaps to Mustique, if it's going to take longer? Some proper sun will do us both good. There's never enough sun here."

That idea was actually tempting, but I couldn't leave now for a multitude of reasons. The most pressing being that I wanted to have filthy, degrading sex with the plasterer for as long as I could. But I also had this report I needed to get done, and the preparations for my heat to make.

There was the board's edict too, but I'd been trying not to think about that. At this point, I was confident that I wouldn't be able to bring myself to do what they wanted me to do, and I'd never be able to look myself in the eye again if I did. Om-Guard would never be mine, and I'd made my peace with that—or I was working on it, at the very least. But I wasn't ready to address the questions that were raised of what was next for my future.

"Perhaps after my heat, Mama."

"Your heat!" she shrieked, making me wince, my gaze darting to the office door to confirm that it was still closed. "Oh Inika, you cannot have this alpha in the house. What are you thinking? You are usually such a sensible girl."

"It's still weeks away, Mama," I assured her, gritting my teeth slightly. "I'm perfectly safe, but I have a lot to accomplish in the lead-up, so a holiday—or even switching homes for a while—isn't practical. Why don't I come around for dinner, Mama? Will that make you feel better?"

She pulled out the thin glass Om-Guard 10ml Scentshield Rollerball tube for the third time in the course of our call, absently coating her pulse points again.

"Yes, that would be good. I'd like that. Your uncles are already coming for dinner. We're having Zafrani Murgh."

"Sounds delicious. I'd love to join you."

I finished the call and logged off my laptop at 2:58, hurriedly mentioning to a tight-lipped Graeme that I didn't want to be disturbed as I darted up the main stairs. The shower in the hallway bathroom was running—probably the reason for Graeme's disapproval—so Blake didn't see me as I inched under scaffolding and around his workspace to open the door to the only room at this end of the house.

It was my own personal version of a professional fuck den. A makeshift but impersonal nest, used purely for fucking, because no alpha would see my real nest except my mate—if I ever decided on one of those. Once I was in the throes of passion and the sheets were soaked in slick and pheromones, I was usually comfortable enough in here, but the lead-up was always an exercise in endurance because it wasn't *my* nest. It smelled like nothing. The upholstery was all chosen by me, but I'd intentionally not selected anything with personality because I didn't want to get attached to it. The room was white, sterile, and functional, but it got me through my heats and the odd dalliance in between, so I couldn't complain.

Confident that none of the staff would venture up here, I left the door open, allowing a clear view of the bed from the under-construction part of the hallway. I kicked off my shoes, sliding them under the bed, and climbed onto the mattress so I could attempt to organise the cushions and blankets into something that made sense to me.

Should I have dressed in something a little more intentionally seductive? I glanced down at my black mini skirt and grey cashmere top. My suite of rooms was next door. I could run over and put on some kind of strappy lace bodysuit. Or perhaps the red corset that pushed my breasts up to my chin?

No, this was better. Even though this encounter *had* been orchestrated in advance, I didn't want it to *feel* orchestrated.

I wanted to feel caught.

Like he'd read my mind, the door clicked shut behind me and I startled, not having heard Blake enter while I was on all fours, tucking in a sheet.

"Don't. Move."

I froze in place, face down, ass up, the linen sheet clutched tightly between my fingers. There was a pulsing, cramping sensation just south of my bellybutton, and I immediately felt my lace mesh knickers grow damp with slick. From two words. No alpha had ever had the effect on my body that this surly plasterer had.

He moved around the side of the bed, so close that I could feel the heat of his body on the backs of my exposed thighs, but he didn't actually touch me. My hips tilted forwards of their own volition, begging without words as my face burned with humiliation at my desperation.

"Remind me of your safe word."

"Audit," I replied breathily.

Calloused fingers traced the outline of my underwear beneath with a featherlight touch. We were silk and sandpaper, and the contrast between us only made me wetter.

With no preamble, Blake pulled the scanty fabric tight, yanking it up so it rubbed against my throbbing clit. I rocked back instantly, gasping for air at the sudden contact.

Blake let out a growl of approval that had my pussy clenching around nothing.

"What a perfect little slut you are, princess."

I came instantly. It was the most humiliating, satisfying orgasm of my life. A few rubs of my clit with my own knickers and the most disrespectful praise I'd ever had the pleasure of hearing, and I was done for.

Blake flipped me onto my back while I was still trembling, manoeuvring me like a rag doll so that I was lying with my hips at the edge of the bed. He tugged off my underwear, tossing them away before bending my legs up so my feet were flat on the mattress, leaving me clothed and yet entirely exposed.

My fingers twisted the sheets on either side of my head as I squirmed my way through each pulse and shake rattling my body, setting my nerves alight.

Blake never took his eyes off my face the entire time, and that made me feel more vulnerable than anything else.

"Pretty," he said gruffly, staring down at me.

The quiet, oddly intimate moment extended before he seemed to shake himself off right in front of me, straightening his spine and pushing his shoulders back.

While Blake's expression appeared to be all bored arrogance at first, the heated desire in his eyes and the thick layer of alpha pheromones in the air were undeniable. He wanted this as much as I did.

Blake bunched up my skirt, gripping the waistband like a handle and keeping me pinned to the mattress like a butterfly beneath a tiger's paw. His pupils dilated as he knelt down, leaning over and inhaling my pussy like it was a particularly fine vintage.

It was lewd in a way that sex never had been for me before. I loved it.

"Fuckkkk," Blake groaned roughly, knuckles kneading into my abs as his hand shifted restlessly. "That fucking *scent*. That's rich girl pussy right there. You gonna let me lick this champagne cunt?"

"I'm going to let you ruin this champagne cunt," I breathed, writhing beneath him, desperate to feel more than just his hot breath on my clit.

I wanted him to be rough with me. To tell me I was spoiled and to make me beg. I wanted to *let go* in every respect and trust him to catch me when I fell.

"Of course you are," Blake agreed easily, parting me with his free hand, exposing my dripping hole.

He flashed me a grin, and my stomach fluttered in a way that I wasn't entirely sure I could attribute to sexual desire.

And yet Blake still didn't touch me where I needed him to. He just watched for a long moment as slick pooled, forming a wet patch under my ass on the sheets. "What a mess you are, hm?"

"Yes," I breathed, trying and failing to squirm in his firm grip. "Yes, I'm so messy."

Blake's gaze travelled slowly up my body, his expression almost bored. "And so *shameless.*"

He tutted disapprovingly and a small, humiliating whine of need escaped me before I could hold it back.

"What's that, princess?"

Use your words. That's what he wanted. Blake wasn't going to do a thing until I pleaded for it.

"Touch me. Use me. *Please.*"

"You are such a good little fuck doll," Blake replied conversationally, using his grip on my skirt to shove me further up the bed. "I want a taste, princess. Feed me."

I slid a hand between my thighs, wetting one finger and holding it up for him to taste, melting from a combination of shame and desire that I'd *begged* for his touch and he'd arrogantly made me touch myself instead.

With a smirk of approval, Blake guided my wrist to his mouth, sucking my finger into his mouth, a rumble of approval vibrating in his chest.

"Fucking expensive," he growled, releasing my digit with a pop. "Just like I thought. You taste like top-shelf whiskey and spoiled little rich girl problems."

I all but sobbed in agreement, feeling more empty than ever.

"Tell me you want me to take those rich girl problems away," Blake purred, cupping my pussy so possessively that I briefly bared my neck before remembering myself. "Tell me you want these rough, working-class hands all over you. In your cunt, in your mouth, around your throat."

Blake's alpha dominance was clear in every word, every movement, but I felt oddly certain that he would never use his bark on me. Seemingly without doing anything, he was making me feel incredibly safe.

"I need you. Only you. Please—"

"Legs up. Hold them in place."

I didn't hesitate, gripping the back of my knees and pulling them up as high as I could, exposing myself entirely.

"Spread those lips for me, princess. I can't do all the work."

"You haven't done any work yet," I muttered, my face burning as I slipped a hand between my legs, shaping my fingers like a V and putting my slick-covered pussy on show.

He cut me an entirely unapologetic grin before looking between my thighs with a sigh that was somehow disappointed, amused, and aroused all at once. It was a potent combination.

"And yet, look how desperate you are for me, princess." He tutted. "Anyone would think you've never had a proper fucking before."

Blake lowered his head slowly, scraping his beard over my inner thigh, coating his face in the scent of my arousal and sparking my own possessive instincts.

Don't get attached. It's just great sexual chemistry. That doesn't mean he's your soulmate.

Though, that resolve grew shaky at the first few confident swipes of Blake's tongue. Maybe he was my soulmate. I liked to believe my soulmate would be as devout of a disciple of pussy eating as Blake was. He was enthusiastic and not at all self-conscious. I was desperate to move, but he kept me pinned in place with my bunched-up skirt, the weight of his forearm bearing down on my hip.

I gasped my way through another soul-blistering orgasm, my hands fisting Blake's hair, though I wasn't sure if I was pulling him close or pushing him away.

He stood up as I floated back to earth, wiping his glistening beard on the back of his hand, his hard cock pressed so tightly against his jeans that it had to be hurting.

"My turn, princess."

Chapter 6

BLAKE

I stripped off as fast as I could remove my clothes without tearing them, and climbed onto the bed, grabbing Inika the moment I was lying down and lifting her on top of me.

She sucked in a breath as her palms landed on my chest to steady herself, looking down at me through hazy eyes.

"You're so strong," she whispered, as though there was anything impressive about me lifting her up. In reality, I had so many alpha hormones coursing through my body right now that I could probably lift a lorry.

Inika's gaze was wide and trusting, and it was too intimate, too intense. The level of attraction I felt for her bordered on too much—I had to channel it into fucking her before I said or did something stupid.

"Get on my cock, omega. Are you going to take this knot?"

Inika's elegant, cream-coloured nails dug into my chest as she nodded, lifting herself up on her knees so I could line myself up with her dripping entrance.

"We'll see," I replied dismissively, knowing how hot it made her. "Ride me well enough to earn it first."

I grabbed her hips, yanking her down roughly and filling her in one thrust. Inika's eyes rolled back, her lips parted on a silent moan. As desperate as I was to see her without that soft, expensive shirt on, I couldn't deny that the fact she was almost fully clothed held its own appeal.

She looked so elegant from the outside. Until you flipped up that little skirt and saw the desperate, needy mess she was underneath.

"Fuck," I rasped as she clenched around me. Hot, wet, *perfect*.

"You feel so good," she slurred, tipping her head back and rolling her hips. Her long dark hair had come loose at some point, and it fell down her back and over her shoulders in silky waves.

"So do you," I replied hoarsely, tightening my hold on her hips so I could bounce her on my cock, and get out of my goddamn feelings.

Why was she having this effect on me?

Had it been so long that I just didn't know how to act around an omega anymore?

Inika scratched fine lines into my skin as I moved her, careful not to draw blood. It was a good thing she was being cautious, because I sure as shit wasn't. I'd never been more at risk of being poisoned by omega blood than I was in this moment because I couldn't drag myself away from *this* omega if I tried.

I adjusted my hold, sliding my hands under her skirt to grip her pert ass cheeks, kneading them roughly with my fingers. For now, I wanted to see her face, but I fully intended to flip her over at some point and see what that ass looked like with my hand prints on them.

"Blake," Inika whined, grinding her clit against my pelvis with each desperate movement, fighting to get closer, chasing her pleasure.

She was so beautiful it was almost painful to look at her. So put-together in public, so abandoned in private.

Everything I would have wanted in a mate back in the brief window of time when having one of my own seemed like a possibility.

If I could have dreamed up my perfect omega, it would have been Inika.

She let out the tiniest growl of frustration, a demand that spoke directly to instincts that had been dormant for years. *Deeper. Harder. More.* She didn't need to articulate the words for me to understand the demand.

I grabbed the back of Inika's knee, rolling us while we were still joined and pushing one leg up towards her shoulder, bracing my body over hers. We were skin to skin, our breath mingling with each exhale.

Inika slid one hand between us, fingers circling her clit as her walls started to flutter around me. But it was the placement of her other hand that made me lose my hold on the orgasm I'd been trying to hold back.

She clasped the back of my *neck*.

While there was no denying who was the dominant one between us, it was still a shockingly dominant hold for an omega to initiate. Especially on an alpha that wasn't *hers*.

And yet I wasn't growling. I wasn't throwing her off. For whatever reason, my alpha instincts had decided that it was completely fine for this omega to handle me like this.

More than fine. Fucking attractive, even.

I came harder than I'd ever come in my life, pushing forwards to lodge my swelling knot inside her. Inika let out a breathy moan, her fingers tightening on my nape.

"Want me to stop?" I asked, forcing myself to still before we were properly locked together.

"No!" Inika dug her heel into the base of my spine, and that was more than enough encouragement for me. We both groaned as I settled into place, the swell of my knot on her hypersensitive inner walls immediately setting off a chain reaction of orgasms that we were both simply along for the ride for.

It wasn't until we were both lying still and panting, with Inika's body draped over me like a blanket, that I remembered just how quiet and intimate the act of knotting an omega was. It had been at least a decade since I'd done it. Neither of us could physically leave—we were bound for however long it would take for my knot to go down, with Inika's heart beating against my chest and her breath tickling my jaw.

Suddenly, I didn't know where to put my hands.

Inika's eyes were closed, but perhaps she could just sense my struggle. She reached out sleepily, grabbing my wrists, encouraging me to rest my hands on her bare ass, beneath where her skirt had ridden up.

I wasn't going to object to that idea.

"Are you freaking out?" she asked, peering up at me through one eye.

"No," I lied.

She patted me on the chest. "I think you're freaking out a little. Don't worry, I'm freaking out a little too. I haven't been knotted in a long time."

"Are you trying to make me feel better?"

"… yes?"

I grunted, fingers flexing against her skin. "I don't want to think about anyone else knotting you."

Inika was quiet for a moment before letting out a bright, sparkling laugh that seemed to travel right through my body. "That's fair enough. I don't want to think about you knotting someone else. Let's just pretend we were both virgins until an hour ago."

I snorted, still absently kneading her flesh. "That was quite the bold introduction to the world of sex, then."

She hummed in agreement. "I mean, if you aren't begging to have your champagne pussy ruined, have you really even lost your virginity?"

I choked on my own saliva, awkwardly coughing for a moment while Inika smiled coyly up at me, dark eyes sparkling with amusement beneath thick, curled lashes.

"Yes, well, we don't do anything by halves," I managed to rasp out eventually. "Was that what you hoped it would be? You didn't use your safe word."

"It was better. What about you? Are you happy—freak-out aside?"

"Yes," I replied gruffly. How could I not be after sex that phenomenal with an omega that beautiful? And she had a sense of humour.

Inika was... likeable in a way I'd never expected her to be.

"Good, because I'd really like to do that again." She paused for a moment, looking up at me with a wicked smirk playing around her lips. "Of course, you can say no and I'll just resume riding my toys in my nest each morning—"

I cut her off with a growl, thrusting just enough to set off another orgasm. "You can fuck the toys if you like, but you're fucking me too, omega."

Obviously, it was only temporary. I was an unmated alpha, and I was convenient, and once the project was done and I wasn't in her space anymore, this would end. But that was fine. I'd enjoy this arrangement for as long as Inika was offering it.

"Not to get super deep and personal," Inika began, panting slightly as she came down from her orgasm. "But why aren't you mated already? It seems crazy to me that you're single."

I frowned down at her guileless face. Was she being serious? "It seems crazy that *I'm* single? You're a wealthy, beautiful, and presumably very in-demand heiress. Where's *your* mate?"

If Inika was the least bit bothered by the question, she didn't show it. "I haven't found anyone I liked enough to commit to yet. I am a very in-demand heiress in some respects, but it's not *me* they want. Anyone born into my situation would receive the same treatment."

I made a vague sound of agreement, feeling oddly disturbed by the idea of Inika being replaceable in her own life. There were plenty of things money could solve in mine, but that wasn't a particular problem I'd ever encountered before.

"So, you're not opposed to the idea of finding a mate? You just haven't found one yet?" I asked.

She shrugged against my chest. "It's complicated, and everyone has so many opinions on it that sometimes I think I'd be better off just opting out of it altogether. What about you?"

"Taking a mate isn't a possibility for me." I didn't want to go into the details of Leo's situation, but I felt like I had to give Inika a little more to go on considering how much she'd shared with me. "My family needs my full attention. It wouldn't be fair on an omega to deal with... all of that."

Inika hummed, looking thoughtful, but I was glad she didn't speak those thoughts out loud. I wasn't sure that I wanted to hear them. Not when the afternoon had been so unusually perfect. I didn't want anything to ruin it now.

"There's a fight tonight," Leo whispered the moment I walked through the door. I tensed, waiting for him to scent Inika on me even though I'd scrubbed myself clean with an indulgent amount of Om-Guard body wash before I'd left. She had Om-Guard to spare. I didn't feel bad about it.

I'd even changed into the spare clothes I kept in the van, which didn't have a trace of omega perfume on them. But the phantom scent of her still followed me around, and I was slightly irrational at the thought of Leo picking up even the vaguest hint of it.

"What did you say?" I asked, realising I hadn't responded to his question. I couldn't even remember what it was.

"There's a fight tonight," Leo repeated, giving me a sideways look.

"Oh, right." I sighed heavily, kicking off my boots before their presence beyond the entry mat summoned Freya. "Your left eye is still swollen shut."

"I could beat those motherfuckers with both eyes closed."

"Don't swear, Daddy," Freya said serenely, skipping out of her bedroom and into the living room opposite. I gave Leo a filthy look, and he grimaced.

"She needs new ballet shoes," he murmured, leaning in close so he wouldn't be overheard. "I don't know what the fuck they make them out of, but they're expensive, Blake. She's outgrown her whole kit. That stretchy thing she wears and the skirt bit. I don't know. I need to win some fights."

I closed my eyes, exhaling heavily. Managing alpha pride was a fine line to walk. I paid all the bills and bought all the groceries, and that was fine with Leo and Dad, so long as no one ever mentioned it. But if I ever offered either of them cash directly, they'd kick off about it.

"You need to get a proper job, Leo. Come back and work with me. I could take on double the amount of work if I had a reliable second pair of hands."

The business had always been more my baby than his, but the plan right from the start had been for Leo to be part of it.

"Because you're doing so well," he scoffed, already stomping away. "No thanks. I'd rather fight a couple of nights a week and get to spend the daytime with my daughter."

A vein in my forehead throbbed. I had a specialised skill, and I charged market-appropriate rates. If I wasn't supporting a kid and two grown alphas, I'd be doing just fine. But Dad couldn't work any longer—and I'd never expect him to—and Freya was a kid. I didn't begrudge her upkeep, even if she wasn't my child.

Leo was the fucking problem. He was absolutely delusional if he thought that this system he had going on now benefitted Freya. He didn't spend the daytime with her. He spent it in bed recovering. And he wasn't making anywhere near enough to actually support the two of them.

Maybe I'd been coddling him too much by never asking anything of him. I couldn't even fathom how difficult it must have been for him to lose Ella—the few years after they were mated and before she'd died had been the only few years I'd genuinely *liked* my brother. She'd made him tolerable with her infectious calm and positivity.

But it had been two years since she'd passed now, and while I understood that he'd carry that grief forever, I couldn't accept how that grief was destroying both his and Freya's futures.

Dad leaned against the doorjamb, a cup of tea in one hand, a chocolate biscuit in the other. "No point arguing with Leo. You know what he's like."

"So we all just have to be held hostage to his whims forever?"

Dad winced. "Not forever. Maybe just a little while longer, son. I know it's hard on you. Losing a mate... it's not easy to come back from."

And I could hardly argue with that, could I? Mum had died a few months after Ella's accident, after a protracted illness. Dad had been closer to Leo even before their mates had died, and they'd bonded again through their grief.

I was the one who didn't get it. Who would never understand. Who had no idea what they were going through.

"Fine, I'll go with him to *Leviathan*. You've got Freya?"

Dad nodded. "Perhaps you could take her to dance class tomorrow. You know Leo won't be in any shape to do it, and she much prefers when you take her out than her slow, old grandad."

"Sure," I sighed, silently farewelling the sleep-in I'd been contemplating having. "I'll take her."

"There's a good lad. Give me a hand with tea, will you? I want to hear all about this new job you've started on this week. Mayfair, did you say it was? Bet it's a posh place."

"Very," I agreed, following him down into the messy kitchen where he would undoubtedly make egg and chips shortly.

"What's the wanker who lives there like?" he laughed.

I cleared my throat, immediately heading for the sink to wash up the day's dishes. "She's an unmated omega."

Dad choked a little on his chocolate biscuit. "You kept that very quiet, son."

"There's nothing really to say," I lied, turning my head to the side and discreetly giving the hoodie Inika hadn't even seen a quick sniff. Definitely no trace of omega on there.

"Well, don't get yourself in trouble is all," Dad said gruffly. "I was a young alpha once. Worked on a building site for an unmated omega customer. It was different times, of course."

I gave him a sidelong look. "What does that mean?"

"Free love and all that." His ears turned red. "I think she might have hired us because there were so many unmated working-class alphas on our crew."

I snorted, scrubbing the sink. "Different times, indeed. I'm extremely confident that had nothing to do with Inika Dara's decision to hire me."

But it might be a large part of why she was fucking me, and that was just fine. It wasn't like it could go anywhere anyway. We may as well enjoy ourselves.

What I wouldn't give to be back there now. To be anywhere but here.

Chapter 7

BLAKE

"Hey Blake," Landon said from the other side of the bar, immediately grabbing a pint glass. "The usual?"

I nodded, exhaling heavily and wondering if I should get a coffee instead to wake me up. The fight was late enough tonight that I'd managed a few hours' sleep first, before Leo had dragged me out of bed, but I was still fucking exhausted and wanted to be just about anywhere other than here.

"There's a new guy tonight." The beta bartender pushed the beer over to me while I patted my pockets, looking for my wallet. "Don't worry, this drink is on the house. You might need it to steady your nerves—the new guy is who Leo is up against."

"Thanks. Is he? Leo didn't mention a new guy." My brother had immediately vanished to greet his "friends" the moment we'd arrived, ignoring me now that he'd been allowed on the premises. They weren't actually his friends—they were punters, and Leo was a good bet, nothing more. Leo's ego didn't allow him to see that, though.

"Leo might not know about it yet. Ronnie only brought the new guy on a couple of hours ago. He's a big bastard."

"So is Leo," I replied, shooting Landon a sharp smile.

"True," Landon conceded, tipping his head in acknowledgement, though he seemed oddly uneasy. He'd worked here for as long as we'd been coming to *Leviathan,* and was pretty hard to rattle.

"You're not convinced?" I asked over the rim of my drink before taking a sip.

Landon shrugged. "Ronnie has been a bit... hasty lately."

"In what way?"

He was clearly uncomfortable talking out of school, and I did my best to look casual and less threatening than Landon probably perceived me as. Unfortunately, there was only so much I could do, by virtue of my size alone. My face probably didn't help, though I didn't mean to look like such an angry fucker all the time.

"Ronnie has been making a lot of business choices that feel a little..." Landon trailed off, absently wiping the same spot in front of him as he mulled it over. "Desperate," he decided on eventually.

I nodded slowly, giving the idea some consideration as Landon was called away to serve another customer.

Rents were up everywhere. This area of London—formerly a grimy shithole—had become something of a trendy hotspot recently, for reasons I would never understand. The underground fight scene had been splintering in recent years, both as the authorities cracked down on it, and legitimate fighting became a more lucrative option.

The writing was probably on the wall for *Leviathan*, and perhaps it had been for a long time, but I hadn't been paying close enough attention. And if I hadn't, then Leo *definitely* hadn't, because his attention span was basically nonexistent.

Could I convince Leo to go legit? He was a bit long in the tooth for it, but maybe he could still get a few years out of it. It would be safer and a steadier source of income than this, at least.

Leo and his competitor climbed into the cage just as I was finishing my beer, and I made my way through the still-forming crowd to speak to my brother.

It wasn't until I climbed onto the narrow lip of the raised cage, holding on to the chain link to keep myself steady, that I got a good look at Leo's opponent.

Landon had been underselling when he'd called him a big bastard. This guy was a *beast*, with a bald head and raised veins *everywhere* beneath tomato-red skin. His teeth were bared already, gaze fixed wholly on Leo, who wasn't backing down in the slightest.

At this rate, they were going to have to start the fight early, given the aggression that was pouring off these two.

This had bad idea written all over it.

"Don't be an idiot, Leo," I murmured, speaking to the back of his head through the fence. "That guy looks practically feral."

Leo grunted in acknowledgement, playing with his mouth guard, but that was all he gave me. I should have known he wouldn't even consider forfeiting, but I was irritated regardless.

He wasn't going to concede, which meant he'd get his ass kicked. Then I'd have to lug him home where he'd be half dead for a week, and entirely useless to Freya. By the time he recovered, he'd be demanding to come back here and do it all over again.

With a huff, I jumped down from the raised cage edge, pushing my way through the throng of people who were now pressing as close as they could to the action, drawn in by the temptation of violence in the air. Ronnie had stationed himself behind the betting table, though he was merely supervising as his staff managed the books.

"Oi, Ronnie. Where'd you find this joker?" I asked, jabbing my thumb over my shoulder at the ring.

"New bloke. Rytis." Ronnie grinned, flashing me a mouthful of gold-capped teeth. "He's from up north somewhere. Domas is vouching for him."

Domas was a weaselly little fuck and all, so that lined up.

"You sure he's good to fight? He looks a little feral."

Ronnie waved his hand dismissively. "That's just his face. You know me, Blake. I'd never put a feral alpha in the ring."

It was *because* I knew Ronnie—on top of what Landon had said—that I didn't believe those words for a second. I elbowed my way back to the ring to where Leo was warming up, wondering if I could talk reason into my idiot brother.

Would Ronnie even know what a feral alpha looked like? Considering it was a side effect of unchecked aggression—which was in large supply here—I hoped he would know the signs. But *Leviathan* was always packed with drunk and happy betas, who had a neutralising effect on all heightened alpha responses.

I was familiar with feral alphas because there sure as fuck weren't any happy betas in the army—not in my platoon, at least. Alphas were usually stationed together and sent to more challenging locations, since we tended to be hardier.

I'd seen plenty of those alphas go feral over the years, and I'd battled hard to keep Leo away from his own brushes with it. Once that dam broke, it could never be pieced back together in quite the same way.

By the time I got back to the ring, the two of them were already touching gloves as the beta ref muttered some low words of warning. He directed them back to their corners before climbing out of the cage himself, wisely avoiding being in an enclosed space with two such clearly aggressive alphas.

There was no dancing around, no feeling each other out. Leo and Rytis immediately launched themselves at each other, furiously trading blows with an honestly embarrassing lack of finesse. Leo wasn't usually so sloppy, but he was feeding off Rytis's aggression, and it was making him hit first, strategize later.

"Focus!" I yelled, wincing as Leo caught a sharp jab to the ribs. Fuck my life. He was going to be a right mopey bastard on the way home. Or comatose. One or the other.

I was relieved to see Leo land a few decent hits of his own, but Rytis didn't even flinch, not even as blood streamed directly into his eye from a reopened cut beneath his eyebrow.

The veins under Rytis's skin had been raised in sharp relief before the fight had even begun, but they'd grown alarmingly pronounced now. His pupils were dilated, and his gaze was wild and frenetic, rather than focused or even generally *aware*. Nothing about Rytis's expression changed, no matter what was happening around him.

Ronnie was ignorant or a liar, because this was a feral alpha.

As they continued to trade blows, the crowd—who'd been enthusiastically cheering every time either of them had landed a hit—were now watching in uncomfortable silence. I doubted they knew enough about feral alphas to know exactly what was wrong, but they knew it was *something*.

The worst part was that Rytis was too far gone for anyone to call the fight off now. His hind brain was totally in control, demanding blood. Demanding submission.

If Leo were smart, he wouldn't antagonise Rytis any further. He'd accept a slightly embarrassing defeat, and walk out of the ring under his own steam, with all of his teeth intact.

Instead, he threw himself forwards, coming at Rytis with everything he had. But going feral gave Rytis both a strength and a stamina advantage. The longer it dragged out, the more Leo's movements grew sluggish and sloppy. As soon as Leo found himself fully on the defensive, I knew that there was no coming back from it.

"Concede, Leo!" I yelled, knowing he wouldn't. Not even when he was clearly struggling to lift his arms any higher than his elbows. Not even when he was obviously too slow to block in time.

Leo took a hard punch to the head, crumbling to the ground like he was made of sand.

I slammed my fist against the chain link reflexively, the noise a loud crash in the eerily quiet club.

Rytis's head lifted, bloodshot eyes locking on me as the next target that needed eliminating, despite the team behind him on his side of the cage, urging him to take some deep breaths. Instead, Rytis started pacing, inching increasingly close to Leo's limp form like an animal guarding its kill.

Fuck's sake. Leo owed me for this one.

"Stupid, moronic brother," I grumbled to myself, ignoring my own alpha instincts that demanded I engage and pushing through the still and uncomfortable crowd. No one stopped me as I jumped over the bar top and yanked the door of the small wall panel between the shelves of bottles, pulling down the lever that manually activated the sprinkler system.

It was instantly chaos. Everyone sprinted for the exits, and the rush kicked the useless alpha bouncers into gear, forcing them to safely funnel patrons up the stairs before they trampled each other. I climbed up on the slippery bar top so I could get a view of the cage where Leo was still lying unmoving in the centre. Rytis was shaking his head, flicking away the water in irritation, which was a positive sign. The water was piercing through the haze enough to annoy him, and his support team was using it to their advantage, shouting for him to leave.

"I'll help you pull Leo out," Landon offered, carefully climbing over the bar top with me as I jumped down.

I nodded in thanks, not having thought that far ahead. Landon was slight and Leo weighed a ton, but I'd drag my brother out of here by the ankles if I had to, and he could goddamn thank me for it tomorrow. It was his fault we were here in the first place.

"You'll fucking pay for that, Blake!" Ronnie yelled as Landon and I passed him. "Anything that needs replacing is coming out of your pocket, Blake—you hear me?"

"Ignore him," Landon shouted over my shoulder. "Ronnie will be fucking cooked if someone dies in the ring, and he knows it."

"Comforting," I snapped.

"Sorry. I didn't mean Leo. He's fine, right? You don't seem worried, and he's made of tough stuff. Anyway, Ronnie is full of shit. We've pulled the sprinklers before for crowd control—the club will be fine."

I didn't particularly care either way, but it was nice of Landon to reassure me. By the time we got to the front, Rytis had already vanished from the ring, and Landon followed me in without hesitation, both of us slipping on the wet padded floor as we made our way over to Leo. It took us several attempts, down on our knees in the rapidly forming puddle, to drag Leo upright, his arms draped over our shoulders, body hanging limp between us.

"Now what?" Landon called, panting with exertion as we made it to the cage opening. I'd genuinely been considering tossing Leo on the floor and hoping for the best, so it was lucky that some of the bouncers decided to pull their fingers out of their arses and give us a hand to lift him down. Someone had shut off the water at some point, but the place was drenched and the staff were running around like headless chickens while Ronnie barked orders at them.

"You parked in your usual spot?" Landon asked. "Ronnie will cool off about the sprinklers—he knew that situation was getting out of hand—but he might not forgive you if you call an ambulance to his property. Negative attention, innit?"

"Leo would be pissed too," I grumbled, directing the small crew of helpers to carry Leo upstairs and out into the carpark where I'd left the van. They held him for me as I cleared a bit of space in the back, throwing down some dropcloths for him to bleed on.

"Need anything else?" Landon asked, watching on as the bouncers loaded Leo into the back. My brother groaned, doing his best to squirm away from them, but clearly in no physical condition to go very far.

"No, thanks. Either he'll be fit enough to get out of the van under his own steam, or he's sleeping in there tonight." I shrugged. It wouldn't be the first time.

Landon nodded, looking apprehensive. Alphas were hard to kill though, Leo would be fine. "I'll let you know when Ronnie cools off."

"I'd appreciate that." I clapped him on the shoulder before closing the back doors and making for the driver's seat. If I had my way, we'd never see *Leviathan* again, but I doubted Leo would have the same takeaway from tonight. He'd probably not only want to come back to the club the moment he regained consciousness, but he'd demand a rematch with Rytis to boot.

His idiocy was exhausting. It always had been, but my patience for it had dropped significantly in the past year.

As I drove home through the quiet streets, ignoring Leo's cursing and pained groans as he came back to the land of the living, it was the image of Inika's face that was at the forefront of my mind. Specifically, that mischievous smile she'd given me when she asked whether I was freaking out.

What would it be like to come home to a mate? To crawl into her nest—crawl between her thighs—and lose ourselves entirely in each other?

"What happened?" Leo groaned, his words thick and slurred. "Did I lose? I fucking had him, I swear. Let's go back. Why'd we leave the club?"

It wasn't like I hadn't considered having a mate in an abstract sense before, but now my brain was unhelpfully supplying Inika's face—and Inika's thighs—to taunt me with the future I would never have.

"Blake! Did you hear me?"

"I heard you," I murmured, keeping my gaze fixed on the road ahead and my head in the clouds. Anywhere but here.

Chapter 8

INIKA

For reasons I didn't want to examine too closely, I found myself standing under the scaffolding on the second floor on Saturday morning, even though I knew Blake wouldn't be back until Monday. The staff weren't cleaning in this part of the house until the work was completed, which I was extra grateful for once I realised that the spare nest still had the distinctive scent of Eau de Alpha and Omega Sex hanging in the air.

Though, that wasn't exactly a surprise, since I'd made no attempt to air it out since our little tryst in there yesterday. I hadn't even stripped the bed. It smelled like us because I'd *wanted* it to smell like us.

It was a little embarrassing in a non-sexy way, but whatever. Alphas smelled good—and Blake smelled *particularly* good. And alpha-omega sex smelled incredible, provided you'd been the alpha or omega engaged in it. It was probably foul for everyone else, but as the staff weren't coming in, I could wallow in my own filth to my heart's content.

Though, I did want to ensure that the bedding was clean for when Blake came back to work on Monday. Just in case we had need of it again.

I grabbed supplies and stripped the bed, lugging the sheets down both flights of stairs to the laundry room, and eyeing the indoor pool guiltily as I went past. It was so much work for the staff to maintain, and while I'd told them countless times that they should feel free to use it as well, none of them ever did, and I only swam in it a few times a year at most. So many of the amenities in this house were wasted on me, and it served to make *me* feel wasteful about having them.

Fortunately, no omega—no matter how stupidly privileged—would let someone else touch their nest supplies, so I at least knew how to operate the washing machine. The rest of the appliances in the house presented slightly more of a challenge.

I grabbed fresh linen and headed back upstairs, not seeing anyone on the way since it was more of a skeleton staff on the weekends, anyway. Usually, I quite liked the added peace and privacy, but I had the odd urge to seek out some human interaction today. Mama would be happy to see me, of course, but dinner last night had already tested my patience on that front. It had been two straight hours of my parents trying to convince me to stay at their house while the renovations were happening. Graeme's fretting had been particularly effective with Mama, who'd been all but hysterical about my lack of compromise by the end of the evening.

I could message the girls and see what they were doing, but they'd just want to talk about Spencer's friend Hugo, and I was even less enthusiastic about that.

Perhaps I was being unfair. He might be lovely. I doubted I'd have one eighth of the chemistry with him that I had with Blake, and he'd probably just want to talk about Om-Guard the entire time, but that was to be expected. One eighth of the chemistry was probably the best I could hope for, in all honesty. Most of the time, I wasn't attracted to the alphas I was set up with at all.

Setting the clean bedding on the armchair in the corner, I sifted through it until I found the fitted sheet. Already, the room smelled significantly less like a sex dungeon, and it was deeply disheartening.

Finding the fitted sheet, I kneeled on the hardwood floor to tuck the sheet under the mattress, pausing at the sight of something under the bed.

A wallet.

It was worn, dark brown leather, with B.A. engraved in gold on the front. I flicked it open, smiling like an idiot at Blake's scowling license photo.

Shoot, he probably needed this. Had he noticed it was missing yet? I had no idea what he got up to in his free time, but I imagined Blake slept in on Saturday mornings and hadn't noticed that it was missing yet.

Then again, he should have noticed last night, right? Perhaps I was stereotyping alphas, but I assumed he went to the pub on a Friday night to let off steam after work with his friends.

Blake was such a mystery. In all honesty, that was probably why I was so interested in him. He was a mysterious, gruff alpha who was good with his hands. And the sex was filthy, and perfectly pushed all of my buttons—both the "tell me I'm pretty ones," and the "call me a slut" ones. That undoubtedly helped.

But once the mystery had worn off, so would my interest. The alphas that were chosen for me had no mystery to begin with, and I always grew frustrated with the ones I chose for myself. In every other area of my life, I felt confident in my ability to make decisions and commit to that path.

Just not love. I couldn't commit on that front for the life of me.

I pulled my phone out of my pocket, pulling up the message thread with Blake and hitting call.

"*Inika?*"

I suppressed a shudder at the sound of Blake's deep, rumbling voice down the phone line. It was *unfair* that he sounded that good.

"Hello. How are you?" I paused for a moment, but he said nothing. Perhaps the mystery wouldn't wear off with Blake, since he was so reticent about speaking. "So sorry to bother you on your day off, but I have your wallet."

He muttered a curse. "*I've been looking for it all morning. I, uh, can't pick it up right now. I'm at my niece's ballet class.*"

He had a niece? And he was close enough with her to take her to dance class?

That was... adorable. Though, I shouldn't have been surprised. He'd said that his family was the reason he wouldn't take a mate. Of course, he was heavily involved with them.

"Whereabouts? I can drop it off. I'm running errands all over the place, anyway."

Or I would be. I mean, I *could*. I had things I could get done today.

Or perhaps I was just nosy and wanted to catch a glimpse of Blake's private life. Which was probably incredibly inappropriate of me, all things considered.

"*I doubt you're running errands in Streatham,*" he replied drily.

I didn't think I'd ever been to Streatham in my life.

"Not specifically, but I need to visit my cousin in Wimbledon," I improvised. That much was true—she'd just had a baby, and I'd been meaning to drop off a gift. I wasn't entirely sure how close Streatham was to Wimbledon, but they seemed vaguely in the same direction.

"*Alright*," Blake said slowly. "*It feels inappropriate to agree—you've probably never been to Streatham in your life. But I can't get away right now, and it would be helpful to have my wallet.*"

"It's really no trouble," I assured him, amused that he'd read me like a book.

He rattled off the address for the dance school, and I committed it to memory as I headed out of the spare room and down the corridor to my suite, making straight for the dressing room.

"I'm on my way! See you shortly." I hung up before Blake could change his mind, sitting down at the vanity to freshen up my make-up and fix the parts of my ponytail that had come loose while I'd been making the bed.

I contemplated changing out of my matching sage-coloured linen top and shorts, but I also didn't want to *look* like I was dressing up. After dithering for a moment, I settled on adding a nice pair of leather sandals and a cute purse, shooting my driver a message as I headed down to the courtyard where he'd bring the car up through the vehicle lift from the garage.

Lúcás greeted me with a slightly wary look, holding the back door open for me to climb in before making his way around to the driver's seat.

"You sure about that address you sent me, Miss?" he asked, watching me through the rearview mirror. "That's, uh, not one of your usual spots."

"No, it's not," I agreed, giving him a cheerful smile before settling into my seat in the back of the car and waiting.

Lúcás didn't report directly to Papa, but I knew he'd gossip about this outing with some of the other staff and it could find its way back to my parents' ears via Graeme.

I'd been living alone for over a decade now, but I only had the illusion of freedom. My parents were still hovering, monitoring my every move until there was an appropriate alpha in my life who they could offload the job onto.

My phone buzzed, and I pulled it out of my purse, silencing it before checking the message.

Stasia: Can't you reactivate your social media profiles? It's strange to not have anything to send to Hugo.

Inika: I deleted them all, sorry.

The last thing I needed was to carry around societal pressure in my pocket—I got plenty of it everywhere else.

Stasia: Inika!!!

Inika: Does this guy actually want to meet me?

Stasia: How can you even ask that? Who wouldn't want to meet you?

That absolutely did not answer my question. I put my phone away, watching out the window as we crossed the river. I was glad that Hugo appeared to be just as apathetic about this whole setup as I was—it would be much worse if he was going into this intending to pursue me before he'd even met me. It was the norm, but it was distressing every time.

"We're here," Lúcás said uneasily, pulling up in front of a dance academy with peeling blue paint that looked like it had seen better days. "You're sure this is the right place?"

"Quite sure." I shot him a quick smile in the rearview mirror, smoothing down my shorts and grabbing my purse.

"I'll wait here."

"Are you sure you're allowed to park here?"

"I'll wait right here," Lúcás repeated stubbornly. Oh well, I could always pay the fine if need be.

Fortunately—considering how long the corridor was with small crowds of parents waiting outside the various classrooms—Blake was waiting near the front, and immediately approached once I pulled open the double doors.

"Hey." He flexed his hands at his sides like he wasn't quite sure what to do with them. It was oddly adorable.

"Hi." I pulled the worn leather wallet out of my purse, handing it to him. "One wallet, as promised."

"Thank you. You really didn't have to come out here." He pocketed the wallet, rocking back on his heels.

"It was no trouble." I was omega-smiling again, trying to put him at ease. Usually, I resisted the urge, but this alpha needed a little soothing, though I didn't go so far as to actually touch him. I doubted he'd appreciate that, surrounded by all these people. "How's the ballet class going?"

"Do you want to see?" Blake blurted out, looking relieved at having a concrete task to latch on to. He was usually so smooth—or at least so in control. This was the first time I'd seen him out of his element. "Freya is just in here."

He led me over to the first door on the left, where the little ballerinas were visible through a windowpane, avidly watching as their teacher gave them an instruction.

"My niece is the one freestyling in the corner," he said drily, and I muffled my laugh behind my hand.

She was the one little ballerina who *wasn't* paying attention. Freya's dark brown curls had escaped her bun, forming a halo around her face, and I was pretty sure her sheer pink dance skirt was on backwards. She looked like she was having the time of her life, boogying away in the corner to the beat of her own drum.

"I'm pretty sure she goes to ballet just for the full-length mirrors," Blake muttered, though there was an affectionate edge to it.

"That's what I enjoyed most about it," I admitted, both of us moving to the side so a parent could peer through the window. "Well, that, and the costumes we got to wear for the shows."

"You did ballet too?"

"I think every omega gets put in ballet lessons, at least for a little while."

Blake grunted. "Freya is an omega. She's been dancing since she was two."

"That's so great that you bring her along. I doubt any of my uncles even knew I did ballet." I gave him another omega-approved smile, trying to come up with a polite way to excuse myself before the moment grew awkward. But before I could, the doors to the classrooms flew open and little dancers streamed out, filling the corridor with noise.

Freya seemed to materialise out of nowhere, popping up at Blake's side and staring up at me with solemn brown eyes.

"What's your name?" she asked, her voice calm and steady—almost unnaturally so for a child, but maybe they were all like that? I didn't spend a great deal of time around them.

"My name is Inika. And you're Freya, right? Your uncle was telling me about you." I crouched down slightly so I could hear her properly in the loud hallway. "How old are you?"

"Five. Did you see me dancing?"

"I did. You danced beautifully."

Her mouth twitched in an almost smile. "Do you like ballet?"

"I love ballet." Well, I loved watching it. I'd been no ballerina myself. "I danced for years."

She narrowed her eyes as though she was assessing me, before nodding her head once, having come to some sort of decision. "Uncle Blake always takes me out for tea and cake after ballet. Do you want to come with us?"

Ah.

Blake's eyes went wide with panic, and I stuttered, trying to come up with a plausible excuse that wouldn't hurt the sweet girl's feelings.

"It's just around the corner," Freya said confidently, grabbing my hand and tugging me down the corridor. "Do you like cake?"

"Of course," I replied faintly, shooting Blake an apologetic look over my shoulder.

"Wait here," Freya instructed, depositing me outside a door with a bunch of parents. "I'm not allowed to wear my ballet shoes outside, or my teacher will get mad."

She darted into what appeared to be a changing room, and I turned to Blake to do damage control.

"It's fine," he said before I could start. "I mean, I can get you out of it—"

"No, no, don't do that. I don't want to hurt her feelings."

Blake didn't quite smile, but I could have sworn he thought about it. "I don't want to put you in an awkward spot, but Freya has already had a rough morning, and it's not shaping up to be a great week..."

"I don't want to add to that. And I'm not in a rush. I can make time for cake," I assured him.

"That's good of you," Blake grunted, hesitating for a moment before continuing. "Freya doesn't really get to spend much time around omegas. Her mum died when she was three."

"I'm so sorry," I breathed, my heart aching at the thought. As my omega traits presented themselves, I'd clung tightly to Mama, relying on her experience to reassure me that each new development was normal. Even though our relationship was complicated, I couldn't fathom how much harder it would have been without her.

Blake shrugged uncomfortably. "She lives with me now, along with my brother and my dad. It's a lot of alphas in one house."

I suspected he was underselling how intense that was, but Freya appeared at that moment with a tracksuit pulled over her leotard, and sparkly purple trainers with the laces undone.

Blake knelt down to help her fix them before carefully tucking the rest of her ballet clothes into her unicorn duffel bag, gruffly telling her how nicely she'd danced today. For reasons that I was choosing to believe were unrelated, there was a weird fluttery feeling around my ribcage.

I shot Lúcás a quick message as we made our way out of the building, letting him know that I'd be a little longer. There was no awkward silence on the short walk because Freya maintained a steady stream of ballet-related chatter as we made our way down the road to a small, old-fashioned cafe.

We placed our orders—Blake insisted on paying—before taking a seat at a table by the window. I half expected Blake to object to Freya's choice of location, given that his gaze kept falling to me before glancing around the room, and this table was particularly on display.

Was I embarrassing him, perhaps? I didn't think I'd been a source of embarrassment to an alpha before. Other than my father. What a novelty.

"So," Freya began, looking at me seriously. She seemed so much older than her years, except for the fact that she was using her fork like a hacksaw to cut into a piece of chocolate mud cake. "What's it like being a grown-up omega?"

Blake choked on his tea, giving me a wide-eyed look as though I was going to discuss heat management theory with a five-year-old.

"It's... fine. There are good things and tricky things about every designation," I replied diplomatically, breaking off a small corner of the very generous slice of carrot cake I'd ordered.

This place was nothing like the kinds of venues I went to for tea and cake. The chairs were wipeable, rather than soft upholstery, and the overhead lighting was probably doing terrible things to the dark circles under my eyes, but the ambience was *nice*. Relaxed. No one was silently judging me out of the corner of their eye.

Well, maybe they were, but it was for a different reason. My linen set, which I thought had been so casual, did somehow seem too dressy compared to everyone else's summer outfits.

"What are the tricky things?" Freya asked before shoving an impressively large piece of cake in her mouth.

Blake still looked genuinely stressed, and under any other circumstances, I'd mess with him, but not when Freya was looking at me so expectantly for an answer. It was wise—and brave—of her to take advantage of the opportunity to grill a "grown-up omega" in person, and I wasn't going to let her down.

"The thing that *I* find the trickiest about being an omega is that sometimes people think they don't have to listen to me. They think omegas can't have good ideas—which is so silly, isn't it? Anyone can have good ideas. But sometimes, people have to be reminded of that."

Freya nodded solemnly. "They think we just care about cushions and stuff. Sierra, in my class, calls me a snail."

My eye twitched at the clearly learned insult. It was a jab not only at an omega's desire not to leave the house, but at the trails of slick we left in our wake, and no kid would say it if they hadn't heard it from somewhere else.

"Tell Sierra to shove her opinions—"

I cleared my throat, cutting Blake off. Not that I knew anything about children, but that didn't *seem* like great advice.

"But I don't listen to Sierra anyway," Freya continued, tipping her chocolate-covered chin up. "Because she says a lot of things that she should keep to herself."

Blake grunted approvingly. "You're a good kid, Freya."

He said it like it baffled him. Like he couldn't possibly understand where that goodness came from.

I wondered if Blake realised it had to be at least a little from him? My uncles sent me limited edition dolls a couple of times a year when I was five. They certainly didn't take me to Saturday morning ballet class, followed by tea and cake.

He was so dedicated to his family. He'd chosen not to take a mate in order to better support them. That wasn't a decision anyone made lightly.

"What job do you do?" Freya asked, accepting the serviette Blake handed her and cleaning her face with limited success. "I'm going to be a vet when I'm grown up."

"You must love animals, then. Do you have any pets?"

"I have a spotted python."

"Oh." I blinked. "That wasn't what I expected you to say."

"I did try to convince her to get a cat," Blake mumbled.

"If I want to pet a cat, I can go to any of the neighbour's houses," Freya sighed, looking at him like the answer was obvious, and a snake was the only viable alternative. She turned her expectant gaze on me, and I realised I hadn't answered her question.

"It's not as exciting as being a vet, I'm afraid. I work on the product planning team for Om-Guard. I help decide what kinds of things we're going to sell in shops," I added clumsily, unaccustomed to explaining my rather dull corporate job to children.

Blake's eyebrows arched. "Oh yeah? I suppose that's the sort of thing someone would usually go to uni for."

Someone, not *you*.

"Absolutely. I have a bachelor's in Life Sciences, and an MBA," I replied airily. Which was true, and kept me on par with my colleagues in terms of higher education. But I knew—*everyone* knew, including Blake—that wasn't why I got the job.

If I'd left school in Year 11, and spent a decade partying in Ibiza and St Tropez, I may very well still be in the exact same role I was in now.

Blake didn't look chastened by my words. If anything, he looked ready to challenge me all over again. It was a good thing I'd worn the painfully thick pre-heat knickers, because that arrogant, mildly confrontational expression really did it for me.

Not a soul on this earth had ever looked at me like that. Like they wanted to drag me over their lap and spank the attitude right out of me.

"My grandad says I have to work really hard at school to go to uni," Freya said, startling me out of my inappropriate thoughts.

"It's a good idea to work hard at anything you try," I told Freya. "And as an omega, sometimes you might have to work a little harder than everyone else. But I believe in you." I winked over the rim of my teacup, ignoring Blake's penetrating gaze.

His phone buzzed on the table, and I watched out of the corner of my eye as he immediately tensed upon reading whatever was on his screen.

"Eat up, Frey. Your dad's wondering where we are," he said eventually, downing his tea in one gulp.

"I'm still eating," she replied mildly, giving Blake a look that dared him to rush her as she took another enormous bite of cake.

I didn't quite hide my smile in time, and Blake turned his long-suffering look on me instead. It was only now that his guard was down that I noticed how tired he looked. He hadn't seemed that exhausted yesterday, even after we'd indulged in some rigorous afternoon cardio together.

Freya seemed more than happy to fill the quiet, and I hummed and agreed and asked questions in all the right places as she covered every subject from what she'd been learning about at school to which dinosaur she would have wanted as a pet. I kept waiting for Freya to ask who I was and how I knew her uncle, but I guessed she didn't particularly care about those details.

It was... nice. I enjoyed the company of children, even if I had some reservations about having any of my own. Mama had nearly died having me, and the subsequent surgeries to save her life meant she'd never been able to have another.

"I'm going to stop eating now because I feel sick," Freya announced, pushing her plate away.

Blake snorted, handing her another small stack of serviettes. "That sounds like a good idea."

I messaged Lúcás as we made our way out of the cafe, letting him know my location and feeling slightly sheepish about it all the while. Having a driver was very normal in my circles, but I could see that it would be considered something of an indulgence basically anywhere outside of that.

"Thanks for answering Freya's questions," Blake said gruffly as Freya skipped ahead to swing around a light post. "And for returning my wallet."

"My pleasure." I hesitated for a moment, not wanting to overstep. "I'm sure Freya has other omegas she can talk to, but I'm always happy to answer any questions she might have if that would be helpful."

I wanted to say more, to express some sympathy for what Freya had gone through, but I suspected it wouldn't be welcome. Blake was too proud for that.

He nodded, watching Freya in silence for a long moment.

"Well, I'll see you Monday then," I said brightly, not wanting to end the morning on an awkward note.

Blake's gaze switched to me, and I felt it travel down my spine, setting every nerve in my body alight. How did he do that with just one look? He was a weapon.

"Do you have thigh-high stockings?" he asked, dropping his voice so low that I could barely make it out.

The mood changed instantly, shifting from awkward politeness to suffocating arousal with just a few words and an intense look.

"Yes," I rasped as my slick-proof knickers fought for their life.

"Wear them on Monday, Inika."

"Okay."

My face hadn't cooled down by the time I slid into the back of the car, and I was desperate to get home, shower, then crawl into the sanctuary of my nest. Both because I needed to decompress after going somewhere new for the first time, and also because I needed several orgasms.

"You okay, Miss?" Lúcás asked, clearing his throat.

"Fine, thank you. Home, please, Lúcás."

"Of course. Graeme called—he wanted to let you know that your father had stopped by because you weren't answering his messages."

I smiled tightly, already pulling my phone out of my purse. "Thank you for letting me know."

Papa: We ran into Stasia at Citrus. She mentioned something about the Marquess of Hastings' son?

Papa: You didn't mention this to us at dinner, Inie? Mama asks why?

Papa: He sounds like an excellent prospect as a mate, Inika! The Board would be very pleased with that outcome. Come for dinner again and we can discuss this. Perhaps you can invite him also?

I sighed, slumping down in my seat. I'd been trying to ignore both the Hugo suggestion and the Board's edict, and now they'd converged and I'd be forced to face both head on.

Not for the first time, I considered walking away from it all. I'd been told so many times that my life was perfect, that I struggled to objectively look at it and assess whether or not I was actually happy in it anymore.

And if I wasn't, what was I meant to do about it?

Chapter 9

BLAKE

Fortunately, I had plenty to do at Inika's house now that the replacement laths were in and the plastering could begin. If I didn't have that to keep my hands occupied during the day, I would have bust into her office like a fucking lunatic and bent her over the desk. The idea had been tempting me—or rather haunting me—all weekend.

Why had Inika come down to Streatham? There was no possible scenario where she needed to *hand deliver* my wallet to me. There was an entire fleet of staff here. She could have tasked any of them with driving out to Streatham if she'd felt so strongly about getting it back to me that day. Or I could have come to her—I would have happily done so after Freya's dance class. I'd told her that, hadn't I?

I'd been mulling it over all weekend, and decided that it was either Inika's way of scoping out the alpha she was sleeping with, or she'd just wanted a little taste of life outside of her gilded mansion. First option was entirely reasonable, though she should have brought someone with her for safety purposes if that was the case. And the second one didn't bother me as much as I thought it would. At no point had Inika made me or Freya feel like zoo animals that she was studying. If the greasy spoon we'd gone to was any different from her usual eateries, she hadn't let on.

In all honestly, she'd been incredible with Freya. The kid had talked about her non-stop ever since, which had made for an awkward conversation with Dad about why we'd been having tea and cake with my posh client on a Saturday morning in Streatham.

The whole thing had got my head so fucking scrambled, I didn't know what to think. Sleeping with her again was either the best idea I'd ever had or the worst.

I cleaned up for the day before trudging to the guest bathroom to shower, scrubbing the plaster off me with a pumice stone. It didn't make me feel clean enough to touch Inika, but she seemed to enjoy having my filthy hands all over her.

It was probably just the novelty of it all, but I wasn't going to question my good fortune.

By the time I emerged, I could hear the sound of the television in the spare room filtering down the empty hallway. She was there. Lounging around, watching TV. The sound activated the alpha urge within me to hunt, to dominate, to *take*. The pretty princess omega was toying with me, and it was working a fucking treat.

Like last time, she'd left the door to the spare bedroom wide open, making my territorial instincts go into overdrive, although there was no one else up here. The very possibility that someone might see her like this made a growl rumble impatiently out of my chest.

Which only deepened at the sight of the thigh-high stockings. Black ones, which she'd paired with a black scrap of a dress that I seriously hoped wasn't meant to be worn out in public.

With a dangerously angelic smile, Inika looked over at me, patting the empty spot on the mattress next to her. "Hi alpha. I'm watching a movie. Want to join me?"

Ah, she wanted to play. I stepped into the room behind her, snicking the door shut.

I could play.

"I'm here to work, Inika."

Inika pulled out her best omega pout, the kind that made me want to wrap her in soft blankets and stuff her full of my thick knot. "You've been working all day. Just for a little bit, alpha. I'm *bored*."

Brat.

I kicked off my shoes, leaving them by the door, before approaching the bed. "Is that why you're dressed like a slut to watch a movie, omega? Because you're *bored*?"

Slick perfumed the air instantly, like her pussy had just been waiting for me to ask the question. To say the magic words.

"Yes."

I snorted, waiting at the edge of the bed while she squirmed restlessly in the centre. "You're going to have to do better than that. I've got things to do, Inika. If you want me to play with your cunt, you're going to need to make it worth my while."

Inika swallowed thickly, turning the television off. "How about a shoulder rub first?"

She uncrossed her legs, spreading them wide and patting the space between them.

The little hellion of an omega wasn't wearing a thing under that ridiculous little dress. I shouldn't have been surprised.

"Princess," I growled, already moving towards her like a magnet was drawing us together. "Look at the mess you've made. There's slick everywhere."

She made a gasping sound of agreement, face flushed and body straining towards me as I kneeled on the bed, despite her best efforts to stay in place and look as though she was the one in charge.

Cute.

I loomed over her, threading my fingers through her hair, and guiding her head back so I could look into her eyes. "I should rub your nose in the mess you've made. Teach you a lesson."

Inika's lips parted slightly, and I pressed my thumb into her mouth with my other hand, maintaining my grip on her hair. Fuck, she was dangerous. Confident, kinky, and perfectly submissive when she wanted to be. The whole fucking package.

But my lifestyle wouldn't let me keep her even if I wanted to. And even if I had time for an omega of my own, this one was several tax brackets out of my league.

"I don't need a shoulder rub. Suck," I ordered, pushing my thumb all the way between her lips. "Show me this mouth is worthy of my cock."

Inika didn't disappoint, immediately sealing her lips around the base of my thumb and hollowing her cheeks, sucking with conviction.

Oh yes. I wanted to feel that on my cock. I wanted it more than I could remember wanting anything in a long time.

Inika let out an unhappy whine as I withdrew my digit, moving my hand to my zipper so I could free my aching cock from the heavy confines of the fabric, roughly fisting my shaft.

The beautiful omega beneath me sat with her stocking-clad legs spread, slick pooling between them, dark eyes hazy with lust, lips parted in anticipation of taking my cock down her throat.

She was a beautiful little wreck, and the only thoughts currently going through her head were the ones that her cunt put there. What would Inika be like during her heat? Fuck, I couldn't think about that, or I'd come in my hand and humiliate myself.

"Fuck my mouth. Please, alpha," Inika said breathily, staring up at me.

"Let's see what you want more," I growled, sliding my cock between her lips, her breath coming out in eager pants as she sucked me down. "Dick or air."

Inika relaxed her jaw instantly, eyes hooded as she took me deep, breathing through her nose. I didn't actually have any intention of depriving her of air, but Inika grabbed my hips before I could pull away, holding me in place, drool spilling down her chin from the corners of her mouth.

"Don't you look pretty?" I murmured, rubbing her jaw with my thumb. "Suck me properly, princess."

Her lips didn't move, but I could have sworn her eyes smiled as she picked up her pace, filling the room with the sound of her enthusiastic attentions. Fuck. I had overestimated my ability to withstand the hurricane that was Inika. I wrapped her ponytail around my fist, tugging her head back because it wasn't her mouth I needed, but Inika dug her nails into my hips, bobbing her head with more urgency.

I growled as I pulled her back, baring my teeth as she flashed me hers, accompanied by a little omega warning growl, no less. My cock throbbed in response.

"Who's in charge here, princess?" I asked, leaning down and nipping the tip of her nose with my teeth.

"You are, alpha." All the tension in her muscles melted away in an instant. "But I'm still going to make you work for that submission."

"I'd be disappointed if you didn't. On your hands and knees, omega." I released her hair, stroking her spine as she shifted into position for me, apparently not in the mood to argue with that request. The silky dress thing slid forwards, and she pulled it over her head in one smooth movement, tossing it aside.

What a *view*. Inika's narrow, toned waist flared out at the hips, curving into a spectacular round ass that I wanted to take a bite out of.

I took my time drinking her in, watching as her pussy grew wetter with each second that ticked by.

"Do you like being bent over like this for me, omega?" I slid a hand between her thighs, roughly cupping her pussy and circling her clit with my middle finger. Inika bucked back against me, her head coming up as her spine dipped down, pushing her ass higher in the air.

"Yes, alpha. I love it."

I bit down hard on my inner cheeks, forcing myself *not* to ask who this pussy belonged to. *This omega doesn't belong to you as much as you want her.*

"Ride my hand," I ordered. Unnecessarily, as Inika already was. "Make yourself come like this. Filthy, shameless, *perfect* omega."

Inika moaned, her fists balling up the sheets on either side of her head as she rocked her hips with increasing urgency. I squeezed the base of my cock, giving my barely swollen knot the pressure it needed, though it was a poor imitation of the real thing.

Slick dripped down my hand, coating my skin as Inika found her release. As much as I wanted to savour the moment, I was too fucking desperate for her. I grabbed Inika's hips, yanked her higher, and buried myself to the hilt in one smooth thrust.

Why did she have to feel like home? It was very inconvenient.

Inika pushed herself up on her hands, arching back like she was trying to get closer. *She wants to be held,* my long dormant instincts commanded, reading her body language. I lifted Inika back against my chest, one arm banded around her waist, the other hand cupping her throat as I bounced her on my cock. I could have sworn that a spot beneath my fingers burned, reminding me exactly where my bite would go if Inika were mine.

"Does that feel good, princess? Have you been craving these filthy hands on you all day?"

Inika whined out some noise of agreement, her nails digging into my forearm as she clung onto me.

"I have. I've been fantasising about you in those thigh-high stockings all fucking weekend."

At some point, we both fell forwards onto the mattress, and I kept her pinned underneath me—careful not to crush her with my full weight—as I rutted her like a fucking beast.

"Is it too much?" I asked, trying to find some semblance of control.

"No!" Inika gasped, arching back into my touch as she clenched around me, her voice cracking as she came. "It's perfect. You're perfect."

I growled some affectionate nonsense in her ear that I hoped neither of us would remember, pressing her into the mattress as my orgasm hit. Inika shifted, bending one leg so I could push in deeper, lodging my knot in place and sending us both into orbit once more.

My fingers tangled with hers, clutching them tightly as we came back down. The way Inika squeezed my knot made my vision go hazy. Had sex always felt this good? Had it just been so long that I'd forgotten?

For a few long moments, we both laid still, trying to catch our breath. There was no awkwardness this time—I had no qualms about putting my hands on every inch of her skin that I could reach.

"We've got to stop meeting like this," Inika said casually, her voice slightly muffled by the mattress.

"Don't make me laugh right now. If I come again, I'll pass out."

"Can you laugh?" she asked dubiously. The little minx.

"As far as I know, though, I'm a little out of practice." Not that I'd ever been *fun*, but I'd been more fun than I was now.

"Well, that's a tantalising challenge," Inika mused, folding her arms beneath her head and lying her cheek on them. Her profile was so elegant, it looked like the gods themselves had carved each plane and contour of her face.

Why was this exquisite woman letting me put my calloused hands all over her?

"Should we talk about what we're doing here?" I asked gruffly. I didn't particularly want to break the spell, but I possessed just enough emotional maturity to know that *not* talking about it would make it worse in the long run. Now that she'd seen my life and met my niece, this thing between us felt more *real* than it had last week.

"Now?" Inika asked, voice thick with amusement. I supposed the timing was a little awkward, considering we were knotted together.

"Maybe this isn't the best time," I agreed.

She laughed lightly, careful to hold herself still. "Are you worried I'm going to get attached?"

"No," I scoffed. There was no possibility of Inika getting attached to *me*.

She hummed, seemingly never offended by my bluntness. "Well, we could always just keep doing what we're doing until one of us doesn't want to do it anymore? My heat is in about a month. I suppose that puts a pretty firm deadline on things."

The appropriate reaction would have been to politely agree with her suggestion and perhaps offer some sympathy that heats were something she had to go through at all—I knew they weren't exactly a picnic for omegas.

But that wasn't the reaction I had.

My cock twitched at the very thought of Inika blind with lust and coated with slick, and that was enough to set her off on another chain of squirming, panting orgasms, undoing any progress my knot had made in deflating as she clenched around me.

"It's flattering that you find that idea sexy," Inika laughed breathlessly when she found her voice, her skin glowing with sweat.

"Yeah, let's never talk about that again," I muttered, my face burning. That was some embarrassing teenage boy shit. I was a grown man. I should be able to hear the word "heat" without my cock standing obnoxiously at attention.

"Fine, fine, I won't tease. Clearly, I'm the only one here with a degradation kink." Inika flashed me a grin over her shoulder, and I *almost* managed a laugh in response. Almost.

Inika grilled me with a series of questions on plastering that seemed designed to get my knot to deflate faster since I couldn't think of many unsexier topics that she could have chosen. Was she trying to help me out?

I'd made assumptions about her before I'd even met her, and not one of them had been that the wealthy heiress to Om-Guard would be *nice*.

I rolled out of bed the moment we could pull apart, heading for the connected bathroom to fetch Inika a wet washcloth and several dry ones for clean up. She had a good sense of humour about it, but knotting was messy work.

"Ms Dara? Ms Dara, are you up here?"

Inika froze, wide-eyed, in the middle of the bed at the sound of the smarmy butler's voice.

"Here," I said in a low voice, tossing her the assortment of towels and quickly pulling on my clothes. "I'll handle it."

"How?" she asked, not looking particularly reassured.

"Ms Dara!" he called, in a far sharper tone than I was happy with.

Who did this fucking guy think he was?

I shoved my feet into my boots, not bothering with the laces, but making sure my zipper was pulled up and my shirt was on properly at least. As quietly as I could, I pulled the door to the spare bedroom shut behind me before making a show of knocking my tools around a bit as the butler—Graeme, wasn't it?—rounded the corner, freezing at the sight of me.

"Mr Alwis. My apologies, I didn't realise you were still here."

The soundproofing in this place must be off the fucking charts.

"Is that why you're going around hollering for the lady of the house?" I asked casually, leaning my shoulder against the wall. "I've been in many a grand house and never seen them run like this."

Graeme straightened, his face turning an interesting shade of puce. "How this house is run is none of your concern."

"Of course not," I agreed, because it seemed to annoy him even more. "It's just odd. I suppose I expected a more professional operation, considering the size of the house and the importance of the lady who lives here, that's all." I shrugged. "Guess you run things differently around here."

"Ms Dara has no complaints about how I run this house," Graeme responded stiffly.

"I doubt she'd tell you if she did. She's very polite, that Ms Dara."

"Indeed." He pursed his lips. "If you'll excuse me, Mr Alwis."

I waited until I heard his footsteps get to the bottom of the stairs before opening the guest room door, finding a fully dressed Inika standing there, having clearly washed away any evidence of us with the gallons of Om-Guard body wash she kept in the attached en suite.

The room still smelled like us at least, which was the only thing keeping my irrational annoyance in check. Obviously, Inika couldn't walk around with my cum dripping down her thighs.

My *brain* said that. My instincts felt differently.

She raised an eyebrow at me, though the corners of her lips twitched like she wanted to smile. "Thank you for traumatising my House Manager."

"Is that what he is?" I asked absently. "I think Freya might be my House Manager."

Inika laughed before remembering she was supposed to be quiet and clapping a hand over her mouth. "I imagine she's stricter than Graeme."

"You're not wrong about that," I agreed. Though if Freya strolled around the house hollering for me the way Graeme had just done for Inika, I could at least tell her to mind her manners. "How come he feels so comfortable yelling for you like that?"

Inika's face flushed. "Graeme used to work for my parents. He's known me since I was born."

"He's your employee, though. Not the other way around. You shouldn't have to hide in your own home, Inika."

"No, I know..."

I didn't push it, since she was clearly uncomfortable as it was. It had certainly given me new insight into this omega, though. Inika carried herself with the confidence of a woman who had everything, but there was far more beneath the surface than what she let on.

And even though looking deeper was completely unnecessary and would probably only make it harder to walk away, I had to know more.

There was no scratching the itch that was Inika. She just burrowed further down into my skin with each moment we spent together.

"I'd better go," I told her gruffly, taking a step back.

She smiled, blowing me a coy kiss that made me realise I'd never kissed her on the mouth, and that was a *travesty*. "Until next time, alpha."

Chapter 10

INIKA

By the time the weekend—and tapas with my friends plus Hugo—rolled around, my water bottle was in my hand at all times to counter the dehydrating effects of producing *so* much slick all week.

Blake had finished each work day in my spare bedroom, contorting me into positions I'd only fantasised about, and knotting me until I was bow-legged.

It made the prospect of tonight's dinner even less appealing. Usually when I was being set up with an alpha, I could at least comfort with myself with the idea that I'd get some decent—good, if I was lucky—sex out of it. But I didn't want to have sex with anyone who wasn't Blake, so that was out of the question.

Like I'd conjured him with my mind, my phone buzzed in my purse while I sat in the back of the car, Lúcas humming happily to himself as we headed for the restaurant.

Blake: Freya was asking after you today. Apparently tea and cake isn't as much of a treat when it's just me.

That was unexpected. While we'd been spending plenty of time together this week, there'd been no communication outside of when Blake was at my house.

Inika: I'm sure that's not true! How was the interpretative ballet class today?

Blake: More interpretive than ever.

I smiled at my phone like an idiot before silencing it and slipping it into my purse as Lúcás pulled up in front of the restaurant. Honestly, I wasn't sure how to reply to that anyway. Did he just want to chat? I was attached to him enough as it was without adding casual messages on top.

Would it be weird to ask if I could take Freya out sometime? Probably. She was just such a fun kid, and I hated the thought of her not having an omega to talk to. She was many years off the most challenging of the omega traits kicking in, but there were still little quirks that baby omegas had to deal with—especially how their environment looked and felt.

I couldn't imagine how difficult that would be with three full-grown alphas in the house. Her brain must be in management mode constantly.

"You're a little underdressed," Ivy said immediately as the hostess guided me into the private room at the back of the restaurant. My friend cast a critical eye over my cropped slacks and silk camisole, which—while on the less glamorous end of my regular dinner outfits—did show off a very alpha-friendly amount of décolletage.

With the agonising strappy stilettos, the drop earrings, and the low bun to highlight my neck, I thought I'd made a decent show of myself. It was a little less overtly sexy than what I'd normally wear to meet an alpha, but I wasn't in the mood to be sexy.

Not for Hugo, at least.

"Well, I'm sure if he likes me enough, he won't mind," I told Ivy, quickly greeting Stasia, who peeled her eyes away from her phone for a couple of seconds to give me an air kiss.

"Well, yes, of course. But... I don't know. You could have made more of an effort," Ivy hedged. "Hugo is a really great fit for you, Inika. Those don't come along very often."

"Oh, don't fuss, Ivy," Brigitte chided. "Inika looks lovely. Doesn't she, Miranda?"

Brigitte's mate nodded once, drumming her nails on the tabletop and looking bored. They'd met while they were at the same elite university, and ran in similar social circles before Brigitte had invited Miranda into her nest. The rest of us never spent much time with her—Miranda had some sort of high-flying finance job, and I suspected she found our social gatherings beyond tedious, though she politely never said.

She never said much of anything.

"Well, Hugo will be here any minute," Ivy continued, smoothing down her navy silk dress as she fretted. "Spencer is bringing him. He's just messaged and said they're around the corner."

"Lovely," I replied, accepting the glass of Amontillado that Stasia's mate, George, handed me.

"I ran into your parents, Inika," Stasia said, managing to hold a conversation while still tapping away on her phone. "Did they say? They had no idea about Hugo! Imagine. You must have been busy if you hadn't had a chance to mention him."

"Yes, well, they're certainly all up to date now." I gave her a tight smile that she didn't see, taking a sip of my sherry. I wanted to go home. My make-up was making my skin itch, and my heels hurt, and every time my earrings brushed against my neck I wanted to rip them out and hurl them across the room.

Part of it was pre-heat symptoms. A larger part of it was my personality.

"They're here! They're here!" Ivy whisper-shouted. "Sit down, Inika. Look natural. No, not there— Around the other side, there's an empty seat there for Hugo too."

"Very subtle," I murmured, moving around the table and taking my allocated seat. Not only would I have Hugo on my left, but Miranda had been assigned the seat to my right. There was no way Ivy hadn't planned that. Even if Hugo was miserable conversation, I'd be forced to speak to him because the alternative was Miranda, who barely said a word.

"You probably should have eased up on the Om-Guard tonight," George volunteered helpfully from across the table. "Let the bloke have a good whiff of unmated omega. That's the best way to nab an alpha."

"George!" Stasia hissed, her face flaming red. "Can you be civilised for once, please?"

He shrugged disinterestedly, taking a long swig of his beer. George was from a new-money family, and had bailed out Stasia's family business—their mating seemed to have been thrown in to sweeten the deal. Of all the couples here, I suspected Stasia and George liked each other the least. There was no missing it in person, though Stasia was always effusive in her praises of him on social media and when he wasn't around.

I pasted a polite smile on my face as a laughing Spencer walked in, clapping the man who could only be Hugo on the back.

He was pretty, I'd give him that. Tall and lean, with brown curly hair that flopped endearingly over one eye, and a warm, friendly smile.

Kind, I decided. He looked like a kind alpha. And more personable than Spencer, who wasn't a bad person, but struggled to make conversation with anyone who wasn't like him. I searched my brain, trying to think if I'd ever met Hugo before, but if we had, the interaction hadn't stood out.

"Everyone, this is Hugo," Spencer announced, gesturing unnecessarily at his friend. "Hugo, this is everyone. I'm sure you've met some of them before, but I'll go around the room, just in case."

That made the first introduction significantly less awkward, though the true test came when Hugo rounded the table to take his seat next to me.

Brigitte kindly started a debate with Stasia about nail technicians, which pulled at least some of the focus away from Hugo and I. The two of them could be loud when they wanted to be, and Ivy couldn't resist being drawn in on that particular topic.

"Hello again," Hugo said, getting comfortable and shooting me a charming smile that probably had alphas, omegas, and betas alike swooning in his presence. "I hear these are the designated seats for singles."

"So it appears," I agreed with a laugh. "Though it's hard to be entirely sure. Everyone is being so subtle about it."

"Aren't they just?" Hugo smiled, pouring himself a glass of water from the jug at the centre of the table. He leaned in, dropping his voice low so he wouldn't be overheard. "I hate to bring this up because I don't want to make dinner awkward, but I'm not interested in any kind of relationship right now. I'm tragically hung up on an ex who thinks she knows what I need better than I know myself, and it would be desperately unfair to inflict my current emotional state on anyone."

I gave him a sympathetic smile. "I'm sorry to hear it. And thank you for being honest with me. I'm a little hung up on someone myself at the moment, but Ivy and Spencer got the idea in their head..."

Hugo flicked a hand dismissively. "No further explanation required. Spencer has always been like a dog with a bone when he gets an idea in his head. I did try to tell him that tonight wasn't the best idea, but he insisted that there was no harm in a casual dinner. And look—perhaps he's right. We can be friends, can't we?"

I smiled into my glass. "Of course."

As far as company went, Hugo could have definitely been worse.

"Are you pining over an ex too?" he asked, still keeping his voice quiet so the others wouldn't bother us.

I shook my head. "A friends-with-benefits arrangement." I paused for a second, taking another sip of my sherry. "Actually, I'm not sure we're close enough to be friends."

Hugo laughed, which had the unfortunate side effect of making Ivy look almost giddy with excitement. Spencer leaned back in his seat, smug and satisfied, probably planning out future holidays that the four of us could take together.

Stasia, Ivy, Brigitte, and I had gone to school together and managed to keep in touch, though it felt like we had less in common with each year that passed. Spencer had been the first mate to join our little circle—their parents were business partners of some kind and had pushed the two of them together at Ivy's first heat. He'd tried and failed for years to convince one of us to take one of his friends as a mate.

"A benefits arrangement then," Hugo mused. "Have you considered trying to befriend them?"

"My thoughts aren't usually that wholesome in his presence."

Hugo laughed again, and I felt slightly bad about it. My friends were probably going to leave here brainstorming what Hugo and I would name our future children just because I happened to be delightful company.

"How are you enjoying being back in London?" I asked, shooting the servers a quick smile of gratitude as they started setting out dishes along the centre of the table.

"Well," Hugo began, grabbing the patatas bravas and holding out the dish for me to take some first. "As I said, I'm still hung up on my ex—who is back in Copenhagen—so that's marred the experience of coming home somewhat. Work wanted me to back in the London office, and my family wanted me back to, you know, take on more responsibility and such."

I nodded, understanding that perfectly.

"Did she not want to leave Copenhagen?"

"I'd have never left if that was the reason. No, we had been planning on moving together, but Kirstine pulled out at the last minute. She's a beta, and has bought into the family rhetoric that she's somehow not good enough for me because of it."

"Was she aware of said family rhetoric? That's a lot of pressure to stand up to."

Hugo winced. "Yes. I thought I'd shielded her from it, but... well, they found a way. I haven't given up, though. One day I'll be the Marquess of Hastings, and then I can do whatever I want."

"Playing the long game? I'll toast to that," I said, lifting my glass. He clinked his against mine and Ivy all but swooned on the other side of the table.

"The long game indeed." He sighed wistfully. "But not *too* long, or Kirstine will move on and I'll lose my mind. What about Mr All-Benefits-No-Friends? Are you playing the long game there?"

Was I?

I gave the idea some serious consideration while helping myself to some croquetas. Was I—even subconsciously—hoping that something was going to develop between Blake and I out of our current arrangement?

"No, I don't think so," I said eventually. "Aside from the fact that he doesn't want a mate—and I can't argue with that, so this is moot anyway—everyone expects me to pick a particular type of mate. From a particular type of family."

"A future marquess, perhaps?" Hugo teased.

"It is rather rude of you to exist, be perfect by everyone else's rules on paper, *not* already be mated, and for neither of us to be interested in the other."

Hugo laughed so loudly that everyone gave up giving us the illusion of privacy, demanding to be let in on the joke. Fortunately, he adeptly redirected them in a firm yet charming way that no people-pleasing omega could have ever pulled off.

Spencer brought up some hideous story from their boarding school days that was probably meant to be charming but would have almost certainly landed anyone from a less affluent family in prison, and I leaned back in my seat, content to just observe.

Mating an alpha like Hugo would cement this life for me. This future. I suspected that the others—or at least Stasia and Ivy—met up a lot without me, because I was the awkward one who didn't have a partner to balance out numbers. My social life would probably flourish if I took The Right Kind of Mate.

But if *this* was what flourishing looked like, I was fine withering.

I *liked* my friends, but we had increasingly less in common. The food was delicious, but the private dining room felt a little suffocating. The ankle straps of my heels felt like they were getting tighter with every second that passed.

Maybe I was just getting old. I wanted to go home to my cosy nest, and my silk pillowcases, and my industrial strength retinol.

If tonight had solidified one thing for me, it was that this wasn't how I wanted to spend my future Saturday nights. I'd already come to terms with giving up Om-Guard, but this was a brand new challenge to face.

Chapter 11

BLAKE

"Why don't you go out today?" Dad suggested, handing me a cup of tea as I walked into the kitchen. "Enjoy your day off. Frey wants to spend the day with me, don't you, Frey?"

"No," she replied, not looking up from her colouring. "I want Uncle Blake to ask his friend, Inika, to come over and play restaurant with me."

"She's not really my friend, Frey," I replied, immediately regretting it as my niece looked up, giving me a sharp-eyed look.

"What is she, then?"

Dad coughed awkwardly, busying himself making toast.

"My... client. I'm doing some work on her house."

"Can't she be your friend, too?"

I took a long sip of my tea, delaying my answer. "I guess so."

Freya nodded, satisfied. "That's good. You don't really have any friends, do you?"

"That's a bit harsh, Frey," Dad laughed.

"He doesn't though," she insisted. "Uncle Blake, you should try being nice to people so they'll be your friend. I ask people to sit with me at lunch and then we play together. Have you tried that?"

I smiled in spite of myself. "I'll give it a go."

"Okay. Ask Inika if she'll come over and then she can sit with you at lunch."

Dad snorted. "You walked right into that one, son."

Apparently so. My phone dinged, and I pulled it out of my pocket as an excuse to get out of the conversation, expecting to find a marketing email.

Inika: I don't suppose you and Freya would like to join me for afternoon tea at The Alinac? I made a booking weeks ago that I'd forgotten all about it.

After a few seconds, another message came through.

Inika: To be clear, I know this is not your thing and that you'll probably hate it. I just thought Freya might enjoy herself.

It sounded fucking awful, but Freya would *love* it. And she never got the chance to do things like that—the concept of a fancy afternoon tea at an expensive hotel had never occurred to me.

Shit, the concept of a regular afternoon tea had never occurred to me.

Blake: Freya would love that. Are you sure? Wouldn't you rather go with friends?

I assumed Inika had those, though she never mentioned them. Maybe it was just because the subject had never come up? I didn't talk about my friends either.

As Freya had astutely pointed out, I didn't have any.

Inika: I'm positive.

She sent me through the details and I exhaled heavily, looking up at Freya who was now decorating her unicorn picture with rainbow stickers.

"You're in luck, Frey. Inika asked if we want to go and have afternoon tea with her today at a nice hotel. You got a pretty dress or something to wear?"

Freya shrieked, tossing the stickers aside and jumping down from the table. "Yes! I'm going to go find it right now. Thank you, Uncle Blake!"

She leaped at me and I caught her with ease, swinging her up so she could wrap her arms around my neck and give me a squeeze before grumbling about my scratchy beard and demanding to be put down again.

The moment she'd vanished into the hall, I was forced to make eye contact with my dad, who was watching me with interest.

"This Inika sounds like a generous client."

I grunted in agreement, suddenly feeling like a guilty schoolboy all over again.

"Anything we need to talk about, son?"

"Not really."

Dad laughed. "Suit yourself. You never did tell me anything. Just be smart. Especially with Freya involved. You know she can be a bit funny around women."

I gave Dad a pointed look. "The kid just wants someone to talk to. And Inika is an omega, and she feels for Freya's situation." I shifted uncomfortably. "She wants to help. She's... nice."

"Thought she was a posh bird?"

"She is. *And* she's nice." Saying the words out loud made me confront the fact that I'd assumed she wasn't. I'd made a lot of assumptions about Inika, and they'd all been wrong. I'd been rude to her right from the moment I'd met her. And for some reason, Inika never seemed to hold it against me.

An odd feeling that may have been guilt settled in the pit of my stomach. I had to do better where Inika was concerned. Not because we were ever going to have any kind of relationship beyond what we had now, but because…

Well, just because she deserved better.

Dad shrugged, looking away at the uncomfortable reminder that Freya didn't have any omegas in her life anymore. "I trust that you know what you're doing. And it'll be a nice treat for Frey. Leo has been… well, he hasn't made much of an effort this week."

That was probably the closest Dad would ever get to criticising my idiot brother, so I made sure to savour it even if it didn't make me feel any better.

Hearing that Leo was acting like a prick didn't make him any less of one. It just reminded me that we were all still suffering for his choices.

A few hours later, we met Inika in the foyer of an expensive-looking hotel that had me wanting to crawl out of my own skin. Freya skipped across the marble floor in her purple party dress and rainbow fairy wings, throwing her arms around Inika's waist like they were old friends.

It made my chest feel strange. Today was a day of strange physical reactions.

"I'm so glad you could make it," Inika said, beaming up at me. She looked ridiculously, effortlessly elegant, in a cream linen dress and dainty gold jewellery that probably cost more than my van. If she thought there was anything weird about Freya's fairy outfit, she didn't say it. In fact, she made a show of admiring her sparkly wings.

"Thank you for inviting us," Freya said solemnly, suddenly remembering her manners.

"Yes. Thanks," I added gruffly because my niece was giving me an expectant look and I was trying to be less of an asshole.

Inika's smile turned coy for a moment, as though she had me all figured out, before we headed over to our table.

Fortunately, Inika seemed perfectly in control and knew how it all worked because I'd have been completely lost in a swanky joint like this. I was slightly jealous that Freya got to eat off the kids afternoon menu. The portions were still stupidly small, but they were less pretentious than the adult versions.

What the fuck did "macerated" even mean? I wasn't sophisticated enough for this.

"Are you enjoying your organic cucumber sandwich?" Inika asked me politely, somehow looking perfectly composed and on the verge of laughter all at once.

"It's my favourite," I deadpanned. "How did you know?"

Inika's smile widened, eyes sparkling mischievously. "One of my many talents. I looked at you and thought 'ah. There's a man who appreciates a bite-sized organic cucumber sandwich,' and what do you know—I was right. I just know you'll adore the cauliflower tartlet."

"Sounds delicious," I replied drily, narrowing my gaze at Inika before eyeing Freya's cheddar cheese on white bread enviously, wondering if she'd would tell me off if we stopped for fish and chips on the way home. How was anyone meant to get full off food this small?

"How was school last week, Freya?" Inika asked, taking her attention off me, which was probably a good thing since I was trying to be on my best behaviour, and the challenging look in her eyes made it difficult.

"Good," Freya replied around a mouthful of bread. "Sierra, in my class, told me I shouldn't be allowed to go to school because omegas should stay home."

Inika frowned. "Well, that's rude. And wrong. What did you say?"

"I told her that I'd punch her in the face like my dad taught me."

I choked on my organic cucumber, spluttering for breath while Inika took an elegant sip of her tea, completely unruffled.

"And what did Sierra say to that?" Inika asked, leaning forwards in her seat.

"That she'd kick me in the face. So I told the teacher that Sierra said she'd kick me in the face but not that I said I'd punch her. And then Sierra got in trouble." My angelic little niece took another bite of her sandwich, looking incredibly proud of herself.

Her poor teacher.

Though, I can see how she'd got away with it. From my own memories of primary school, little omegas were able to get away with murder. Even as children, they knew exactly which heartstrings to pull.

"That was smart," Inika said approvingly. "If not a little sneaky. Though, don't actually punch her in the face because then you'll get in trouble. Unless you *really* have to."

She looked expectantly at me, daring me to contradict her words, but I shrugged. Omegas *should* use every tool in their arsenal as far as I was concerned—they had plenty of obstacles in their path already.

Though I was going to verify once we got home that Freya actually *did* know how to throw a punch, because I wouldn't have put it past Leo not to teach her properly.

"Did you go to school?" Freya asked Inika. "In the olden days?"

Inika nodded, not missing a beat. "I did. I went to an omega boarding school back in the olden days. That's where you live at school—you sleep there and everything."

"How old were you?"

Inika glanced at me, probably wondering at the sharp tone of my question as she took a sip of her tea.

"I started boarding at Anworth Hall from age seven, and stayed there until I finished secondary school. Most of my childhood memories were made there."

"Didn't you miss home?" Freya asked, wide-eyed.

"I went home on weekends fairly often, and for school holidays. Though, when I did, I missed my friends and the House Parent a lot because I was so used to being around them."

"It wasn't difficult living with so many omegas?" I asked.

"They're set up for it—everyone has their own private room. And while the school itself is ancient, the ventilation system is state-of-the art," she added, the corners of her mouth tipping up. "I don't think I'd be able to do it if I had children, but it wasn't terrible. And my parents travelled so much back then that it made sense."

I took a generous gulp of whatever disgusting flower tea was in my cup for my suddenly dry mouth. The idea of Inika having children with someone else made my skin feel too tight for my body. I didn't even *want* kids of my own—helping with Freya was more than enough for me.

But apparently my alpha hindbrain heard "if I had children" and supplied "must breed her" in response.

Fuck my life.

Fortunately, I wasn't expected to contribute much to the conversation because Freya had years' worth of questions she wanted to ask. Inika ordered every flavour of tea Freya so much as hinted at wanting to try, and I didn't even know how she paid for afternoon tea because I didn't see her do it, but she casually mentioned that it was taken care of on our way out of the building. It must have been some kind of omega magic, because she managed to say it without triggering some idiotic alpha pride instinct.

Or my idiotic alpha instincts were still preoccupied with the idea of Inika meeting someone and settling down someday. Even though *of course* she was going to do that.

"Did your driver drop you here?" I asked Inika as we left the hotel.

She gave me a sidelong look. "It's a fifteen minute walk, Blake. Even I'm not that pampered."

I snorted. "My mistake. We'll walk you home."

"You don't have to do that."

I huffed impatiently and she tipped her chin down to hide her smile. Chivalry didn't come naturally to me, but there was no way I was letting her walk home alone.

"Can we go to the playground?" Freya asked excitedly, looking wide-eyed at the elaborate setup across the road which was already crawling with children.

"I'm in no rush," Inika volunteered. "I mean, I could just walk home alone, but I suspect you're going to get all alpha about that. I don't mind waiting while Freya has a play."

"If you're sure," I said, grabbing Freya's hand before she could sprint directly into traffic and leading her towards the crossing. "She has a radar for playgrounds."

Inika laughed, buttoning her cream cardigan against the faint chill in the wind as we crossed the road. The moment we were safely on the other side, Freya shot ahead as if we didn't exist.

"It's probably not the worst idea to run off some energy. She sat so politely at afternoon tea," Inika said, watching Freya fondly as her fairy wings flopped lopsidedly behind her.

"She did," I agreed, proud of how well-behaved she'd been, considering she was being raised by wolves. "Thanks again for inviting us. I think this might be something Freya remembers for the rest of her life."

I got the briefest hint of pure contentment from Inika's scent before she pulled out a glass tube of Om-Guard from her purse and began rolling it on her pulse points. I irrationally wanted to snatch it out of her hand and throw it away.

Inika covering up her joy just seemed *wrong*.

"I've been thinking, and I, er, owe you an apology," I said quietly, while Freya made a beeline for the swings.

"Me? Why?"

I frowned, looking at Inika out of the corner of my eye. "For being a dick?"

She dragged her lower lip between her teeth, valiantly trying not to smile. "I assumed that was just your personality."

"It is. I'm sorry about it."

This time, she did laugh. Suddenly, the sun felt a little warmer.

"Don't be. I like to think I'm quite secure in myself—it takes a lot to hurt my feelings. And I like your personality. You're refreshingly honest. Refreshing honesty is in short supply in my life."

"Too many people telling you what you want to hear?"

She hummed in agreement. "It's not their fault, of course. Most of the people I interact with are either on my payroll or Om-Guard's. It would be unreasonable to expect them to speak freely around me."

"You must have friends, right?"

We both fell silent for a moment as Freya sprinted up to me, shoving the fairy wings she'd insisted on wearing into my hands before booking it towards the slide.

"I do." Inika was quiet and thoughtful for a moment, and I watched her with probably too much intensity, hanging on her every word. "My closest friends are the ones I grew up with at Anworth Hall. But they've all found mates, and most of them have had children. We're in different places in life."

"Do you not…" I cleared my throat. "Do you not want those things?"

"Yes and no. My mama nearly died having me. She instilled a fear of childbirth in me since I was old enough to talk, though she regrets it now that I'm not giving her any grandchildren. I'd like a mate—if I could choose him for love, and he cared about more than just breeding me."

A shudder ran down my spine at the sordid term. "Play fair, princess. We're out in public. I don't even want kids, but when you say shit like that, I at least want to practice making them with you."

She snorted, bumping my biceps with her shoulder. "Blake! I can't take you anywhere."

Fuck. What did it mean that I wanted her to? I wanted to tease her in public, and I wanted her to roll her eyes at me then beg me to fuck her the moment we were alone.

It's just because you can't have her, I reminded myself. It'd never work out in real life. You're not going to take her to *Leviathan*. She's not going to take you to her high society events.

There's no world in which Blake Alwis and Inika Dara made sense together, no matter how tempting the idea was.

Chapter 12

INIKA

"Hey," Maia said, poking her head around my office door without knocking. "Do you need me today?"

I minimised the team chat I'd been idly scrolling through.

"No?" I mused. "I'm just answering some emails, then I'm taking a Pilates break."

Maia nodded slowly. "Do you actually need an assistant?"

"Probably not," I admitted. "Not these days. But you get paid for it and a free place to live, so you're welcome to keep the role in name only if you like."

Maia narrowed her eyes at me. "What's the catch?"

"Occasionally making phone calls for me. You know how I despise those."

Maia smirked. "Of course. How do you have such a cool, calm reputation in the media? If only they knew you were deathly afraid of the phone."

"That would ruin the mystery. Are you going into the office?"

"I think I will. Do you want to come? They have hot desks, you know."

I wrinkled my nose. "Why would I want to do that?"

Maia laughed. "Social interaction. Isn't that something omegas crave?"

"Not this omega, I assure you."

"Have you been avoiding us?" Stasia asked while Ivy bounced on the balls of her feet next to her in the foyer of the Pilates studio.

Brigitte, the only one who'd been in class with me, shot me a guilty look. "I may have mentioned where we were going to be this morning."

"We've got a table at Bite," Ivy said excitedly, mentioning the eatery around the corner. "So we can go and discuss Saturday night. We wanted to do it sooner, but you've been *so* hard to get hold of."

"I'm not really dressed for Bite," I replied, scrambling for an excuse not to go.

"Nonsense, I love this set—you look cute. Plenty of people go straight to Bite after a workout. Come on! We've got a surprise for you," Stasia added in a conspiratorial tone.

Great. I wondered what they'd told poor Hugo to rope him into this.

But no, it was far worse than that.

Instead of encountering a sheepish-but-amused Hugo, I found my parents sitting at the table at Bite, sipping their chai and watching me expectantly.

Well, Papa was watching me expectantly.

Mama looked on the verge of fainting, appalled that I'd come to brunch in my forest-green leggings and matching crop top.

"Sit, sit, sit," Stasia said, gesturing for me to take the seat opposite my parents. "Have you had the chia bowl here? It's to die for."

"Sounds great," I murmured, not having the mental capacity to even think about reading the menu.

The claustrophobic feeling I'd been trying to shrug off on Saturday night was amplified by a thousand now, with everyone looking at me, the weight of expectation bearing down heavily on me.

It had been surprisingly easy to reconcile the fact that the future I'd been prepared for wasn't in the cards for me—I was hardly the first of the rich kids set to be dissatisfied with my life of immense privilege. I was just doing it a little later, rather than dropping out of uni and moving to Thailand to find myself after a week-long bender like many of my peers had.

Unfortunately, disappointing the people that I cared about was probably a more challenging ask now that my prefrontal lobe had finished developing and I understood consequences. In hindsight, I should have got all my screwing up out of my system when I was twenty and set the bar lower.

Papa ordered for me while Brigitte valiantly made small talk, her omega urge to soothe out in full force since she was paying the closest attention to me.

What was Blake doing right now?

He was up on the scaffold probably, hard at work. I'd mentioned that I wouldn't mind if he used a speaker to listen to music, noticing that he didn't wear headphones and wondering if he found them uncomfortable, but he'd declined. It was another thing that made him oddly attractive to me. I needed external stimuli to distract me from the relentless stream of noise in my head. Blake was content to just *be*.

"You can't put it off any longer," Ivy laughed, giving my hand on the table a light squeeze. "We want to hear all about Saturday!"

"You were there," I pointed out mildly.

"We weren't," Papa countered. "But your friends have told me all about this Hugo fellow. Inika, he sounds very good. A nice young man."

Mama nodded, absently rolling Om-Guard on her wrists and staring at my workout top like she could transform it into a modest silk blouse if she just glared at it hard enough.

"He is a nice young man," I agreed, suspecting that Hugo was staring down the barrel of forty, but that would be considered young in Papa's eyes. "We got along very well. We could be great friends I think."

It was almost impressive, the way disappointment fell around the table like a veil descending. My ability to ruin the mood might have been my superpower.

"Friend?" Ivy repeated with a nervous giggle. "I mean, all the best matings are rooted in friendship…"

"You know that's not what she meant," Brigitte mumbled, stirring her tea a little more aggressively than necessary.

"Did any of you actually speak to Hugo?" I asked, raising an eyebrow as I surveyed the table. "I assure you, we're quite on the same page about this."

"But you got along so *well*," Stasia all but wailed. "The two of you were laughing all night!"

"Well, yes." I frowned. "That's because I'm funny."

Not that Hugo was *un*funny, but I'd been the one really bringing the jokes.

"Inika," Ivy all but pleaded. "Please don't rule him out. You haven't even given him a chance! Your father mentioned what the Om-Guard Board said…"

I gave Papa an accusing look, and he had the grace to look at least a little embarrassed.

"Hugo would be *perfect*," Stasia added, a dreamy look on her face. "You've only got a couple of weeks haven't you?"

"Stasia," Brigitte scolded. It was poor form to bring up my impending heat in general, let alone in a public cafe.

"I know, I know, but this is an emergency," Stasia sighed. "We need to have a frank conversation here, B. Before Inika makes the worst mistake of her life."

Was this an intervention? Perhaps it hadn't started out that way, but that was the direction it had gone in.

"Inika is thirty-four, and more than capable of making her own decisions," I reminded them gently, rolling my neck and trying to repress the omega urge to roll over and submit. To make the tension go away by any means necessary.

If there was ever a time to fight against that instinct, it was now.

"We know, darling," Papa said gently, his eyes sad. "But you have been ignoring your responsibilities for so long. And perhaps that is my fault, for not being firmer with you. But I'm afraid I might have to be now."

Mama clasped his hand, dabbing her eyes with the other.

I was a reasonable person. I was. I didn't like making a fuss. Calm and collected was my default state of being.

But there was a strange, hot, itchy feeling crawling up my spine that might have been rage.

"Invite this Hugo home for dinner to meet us. Court him properly, Inie. If you truly feel in your heart that he would be a cruel mate to you, then of course, you should not invite him to your nest. But if he is a nice alpha, if he is kind, and behaves as a man in his position ought to, then I cannot abide by you not doing everything within your power to secure such a match."

"We're just all ignoring the part where he's not interested, are we?" I asked drily. Or at least that was the tone I was aiming for, though I suspected some of the bitterness I was feeling leaked through.

Apparently we *were* all ignoring that, since no one acknowledged I'd spoken.

"Inika, if you want to maintain the lifestyle you have—" Papa began as my friends gasped at the threat of me being disinherited. And to give my parents a small amount of credit, I supposed, they looked pained by the words Papa was saying.

But he was still threatening me, so I wasn't feeling overly charitable about it.

"Noted," I cut in, pushing out of my seat. "If you'll excuse me, I have places I need to be."

The weight of alpha disapproval and omega distress felt like an anchor, physically dragging me down with each step forwards I took, but I pushed on regardless. This was a conversation that had been a long time coming, and I'd needed to have it, no matter how painful it felt to let everyone down.

Whatever choices I made from here on out, whatever happened, the decisions were going to be mine. The mistakes were going to be mine.

And hopefully, I'd find some joy in there too.

I didn't wait for Lúcás to collect me, hailing a cab instead to make the short trip home. It was only once I was home and helping myself to a glass of water in the kitchen that I finally pulled my phone out of my purse, unable to resist reading the messages that would undoubtedly hurt my feelings.

Before I could, an incoming call flashed on the screen.

"Ms Dara? It's Annelise here from Prendre."

"Hi, Annelise. How are you?" I asked, balancing the phone between my ear and my shoulder as I poured more water. A definite sign that my heat was approaching—I was always *so* thirsty in the lead-up.

"Fine, thank you. I was just calling as we really need to set up some interviews for you for your next session with us." Session was such a polite way of saying week-long fuck fest. *"Would you like us to come to you as we did last year?"*

"That would be best, please." The last thing I needed was for someone to see me walking into the Prendre building. It was far more discrete to have them visit me here for interviews.

"Excellent, I'll send through some times as options. Was there anyone in particular you were hoping for?"

"No, no one in particular." I'd never had the same alpha for my heats twice, even if they were available. Using a temporary alpha was already a dangerous game to play when it came to my heart—there was no time more vulnerable for an omega than their heat. I took as many precautions as possible.

There was a strange, uncomfortable feeling in my gut, that I wanted to ignore but I knew wouldn't go away. It was a Blake-flavoured feeling. He was the alpha I wanted—the *only* alpha I wanted.

"I'll put together a short list then, based on what you've said you liked in previous years. And, of course, if you'd like us to simply facilitate with an alpha of your choosing outside of Prendre, that's a service we offer as well."

An alpha...

"Right," I stuttered, having forgotten all about that. I'd never even contemplated that service offering in the past.

"I'll be in touch with some names and times to meet. Have a lovely day, Ms Dara."

I hung up, slightly on autopilot as I made my way out of the kitchen.

An alpha of your choosing.

Okay, Blake didn't want a mate, but *maybe* he wouldn't be opposed to spending my heat with me? If it was any other alpha, I'd worry that they'd want to save that experience for their future mate, but if Blake didn't plan on taking one... Well, this might be his only opportunity. And while heats were kind of a liability, there was fun to be had too.

I could ask the question. It couldn't hurt to ask. And now seemed like an opportune moment—there was no one else around, and we were both clear-headed and not distracted by impending sex. Then again, I'd be interrupting Blake when he was working, which was probably poor form on my part.

I dithered in the hallway once I'd finished dragging myself up the stairs, trying to decide what to do.

Was this a decision rooted in logic? Or was I emotional and reactive after this morning?

Maybe I should leave. Go and shower off the pilates sweat and stress pheromones at the very least. I could talk to him later.

"What are you doing, Inika?" Blake called from around the corner.

Well, that solved that dilemma.

"I was coming to talk to you," I replied, hobbling around the corner as my calves chose that moment to start throbbing, but trying to make it look smooth.

The sight of the progress Blake had made this morning had me halting in my tracks, my woes briefly forgotten.

Where the low false ceiling had been was now a smooth, arched plaster masterpiece. This one small section of the house looked like it had been taken from a museum and seamlessly integrated into the house. Or perhaps it was the opposite, since the curved arch ceiling had been part of the original design.

It looked like Blake had peeled away a facade, highlighting the beauty underneath.

"It looks amazing in here," I said, staring up at the progress. "So much better than I could have even visualised from the plans."

Blake nodded silently, eyeing one spot in a particularly critical way. "It's certainly an improvement over what was here."

"It's more than just an improvement. You're really talented, Blake."

He raised an eyebrow at me. "What's with all the compliments?"

"They're genuine compliments!" I nudged his biceps with my shoulder. "You're just bad at taking them."

His beard twitched in a half smile. "That's probably true. Was there something you wanted to talk to me about?" he asked. "Or were you coming to inspect my craftsmanship again?"

I blushed at the reminder of how we'd got into this whole arrangement in the first place. "I've been very slack on the work inspection front, but no, I did have something I wanted to discuss." I smoothed the waistband of my leggings, feeling oddly nervous. Was this a good idea? I'd always wonder if I *didn't* ask. "You recall that I mentioned my heat was approaching?"

Blake gave me a sidelong look. "I remember."

His voice seemed to have dropped an octave, and I did my best to tamp down my reaction at the reminder of how enthusiastically he'd responded to the mention of my heat the last time we discussed it.

"Right." I exhaled heavily. "I'm just going to come out and say it—"

"I can't take a mate," Blake blurted out, his face flushing. "If that's what you're going to ask. I wouldn't... I wouldn't treat her right. I wouldn't be able to make her a priority."

Maybe I wasn't ready to go out into the world and make my own mistakes. Maybe I should crawl back to my parents and let them make the mistakes for me.

No. No. I could do this. While I understood why his mind had gone there first, I was still slightly startled by the assumption. If I ever asked an alpha to accompany me to my nest for the purpose of becoming my mate, I'd do it in a slightly more romantic setting than this.

"I... know. No, I know. Well, I don't necessarily think that's true, but never mind. That wasn't what I was going to ask you."

"Right." Blake cleared his throat, his cheeks flushing. "Sorry. I shouldn't have assumed."

"No, no, don't apologise. I know it's standard practice for omegas to spend their heats alone if they're unmated, but I usually... don't."

Blake frowned. "What does that mean?"

I hadn't thought this through. Actually explaining the concept of Prendre to Blake was a mortifying proposition. "There are, well, services available. Alphas who make themselves available to help omegas during their heats."

I'd never seen Blake's eyes go so wide. He generally wasn't so expressive.

"The service includes a support crew to keep the alpha safe. The alpha and the omega both wear muzzles for the duration. There's a nurse on hand too to administer the postcoital contraception shot directly after the heat to ensure there's no pregnancy. That kind of thing."

"It sounds..." He trailed off, looking slightly lost for words. "I've never heard of anything like that."

I cleared my throat. "It's prohibitively expensive for the vast majority of people. And many would find it... wrong, I guess. For some people, heats are meant to be these sacred moments between mates."

"Not you?"

Oddly, no one had ever asked me that quite so directly before. My parents knew I used an agency, and they hated it but also hated the idea of me suffering which seemed to cancel it out. Most of my friends kept their disapproval to themselves, especially since it was such a taboo subject to begin with. And the only other people who knew about it were my staff, who weren't going to be honest with me anyway.

"Maybe it's just because I'm a pampered little omega heiress, but I don't see any virtue in suffering when I don't have to." I shrugged. If that made me spoiled or high maintenance or out of touch, then I guessed that I just was all of those things. "Going through heat alone is awful, but committing to a life with someone just to have a partner for it is an even worse prospect. I'm able to afford this service, so I make the most of it."

Blake nodded slowly, his brow furrowed. "I guess that makes sense. And you wanted to discuss that with... me?"

The intention of my ill-thought-out plan had been to frame the idea as something that could be fun for both of us. But seeing the confused and not at all horny look on his face had me wondering if the offer would come across as kind of insulting. The sex we were having right now was a mutually beneficial arrangement. Servicing me through my heat was just that—a service. Just because the alphas enjoyed themselves didn't mean it wasn't hard work.

And I didn't want him to think I thought of him as *just* good for sex, even if a relationship between us was never possible. I liked Blake's company. I respected him.

He meant something to me, despite my best intentions.

I took a step back, soothing omega smile in place. "You know, never mind. I don't think I've gone about this the right way—"

"Ask the question, princess," Blake commanded softly, using the voice he used in bed which was so patently unfair. I was helpless against that.

"If you wanted to be that alpha in the room, in the *nest*... It can be arranged. That's all. They can give you a briefing and put the various safety measures in place to make sure you can't bite me, and they provide a support crew for your comfort. Okay, well that's all I wanted to say. I'm going to go crawl into a hole and die now."

"No, you're not." Blake reached for me before I could turn away, pulling me in close. He was covered in plaster dust, and it immediately coated my clothes, but I didn't care.

I was getting a *hug*. Blake and I didn't hug. I mean, maybe post-sex, but we were literally stuck together then, so it'd be awkward if he put his hands anywhere except around me.

"Thank you, Inika. I'm glad you thought of me, and I'm glad you were brave enough to ask. But I can't take five days away from my family, as much as I would very much like to."

I nodded against his chest. *Inika, you idiot.* Of course, he wasn't going to just abandon Freya for five days.

He sighed. "This is the *only* time I've been tempted to take some time away from them, though. You're hard to say no to."

"I probably shouldn't have asked."

"I'm glad you did."

We stayed there for a long moment, and it felt so different from our usual interactions that I wasn't quite sure what to make of it.

Blake sighed heavily, his breath ruffling my hair. "I really misjudged you when we first met."

I smiled against his chest. "I'm not upset about it. I imagine you've met a lot of clients like me in your time."

"I've never met anyone like you, Inika."

I didn't quite know what to make of that, and even though I'd applied more Om-Guard on the cab ride home to mask the stress smell, I was worried that my scent would give away my reaction. Blake's hands lingered on my hips as I stepped back, his eyes looking critically over my outfit as if he hadn't just said something that had the power to decimate my heart. "I've got you all dirty. Not in the fun way this time."

"Hugs are fun." I was impressed at how light I managed to keep my tone. "And I need a shower anyway. I just went to Pilates."

"Did you now?" Blake asked, his gaze lingering on my leggings like he'd just noticed I was wearing them. Back to flirty. Back to horny. This was much safer ground for us. I knew how this went.

"Mmhm. My poor calf muscles are aching. And my glutes..." I sighed dramatically, switching my body language from reserved to fuck-me in an instant. "I think I need a massage."

"I'll keep that in mind for later," Blake said with an easy wink, releasing me and picking up his tools again. "Until then, princess."

Well, I'd wanted to own my own mistakes, and I'd successfully made the first one.

Chapter 13

BLAKE

How the fuck was I meant to focus on anything else when Inika had come to me and asked me to fuck her through her heat?

The entire day was a write-off.

Fortunately, my task today was creating the decorative ceiling boss that sat in the central point of the arches, which was fiddly enough to make time pass quickly, but artistic enough that it didn't demand perfection the way the smooth plasterwork on the ceiling did.

By quarter to three, I was showered and ready, eagerly awaiting Inika's arrival in the spare room.

Leo: Can you watch Freya tonight?

I exhaled heavily, regretting checking my phone at all.

Blake: Why?

Leo: There's a new club just opened up that I want to visit.

Ah. He hadn't been able to build bridges with Ronnie again then. *Good.* Then again, there was always a chance that whatever hole he was heading to tonight was even worse than *Leviathan.*

Leo: If you say no, Dad will cancel his plans to have dinner with Jasper.

Manipulative little fuck.

Blake: Fine.

Dad deserved a night off—or several. He was retired and his kids were grown. Instead, he probably did at least as much child rearing now as he'd done when Leo and I were young, considering Mum had been our primary caregiver.

Inika let herself into the room quietly, wearing a loose-fitting black dress that I was convinced was hiding some elaborate lace contraption underneath, though I didn't know where that idea had come from.

Immediately, I was aware that Inika's body language wasn't as relaxed as it usually was. Her smile was there, but it was a little less sure than normal. Her scent wasn't broadcasting distress, but she didn't have slick pooling in her knickers yet either.

Of course not, you fucking asshole. You rejected her this morning.

I hadn't necessarily thought of it as a rejection at the time. It wasn't as though I didn't *want* to spend Inika's heat with her—I did. More than anything. But five days away would be an unfair burden to place on Dad, who'd have to pick up Leo's slack all on his own.

"Come here," I said gently, opening my arms and waiting for Inika to close the distance between us. I was rusty as fuck when it came to providing comfort—if I'd ever had the skill in the first place—but I'd try for her.

She walked into my embrace like it was the most natural thing in the world, and I grabbed her waist, lifting her up until she wrapped her arms and legs around me, clinging on like a koala.

"What are you wearing, hm?" I murmured teasingly, shifting my arms to beneath her ass to support her. Whatever she had on under that loose dress felt very... structured.

"Slutty corset," Inika mumbled.

"Sounds delightful."

She leaned back so she could look into my eyes, shifting her weight to my arms, entirely confident that I would hold her steady.

"Are you okay?" I asked.

Inika pursed her lips, looking considering. "Yes. I think."

I walked us over to the bed, sitting down on the edge while Inika adjusted her position to sit more securely on my lap.

"Is it about our conversation this morning?"

"A little, but not entirely. I had a difficult conversation with my friends and my parents this morning. Setting boundaries, I suppose. Asserting a little more authority over my own life."

"How did that go?" I asked, feeling oddly proud. That wasn't an easy task for any omega to undertake, and I imagined it was even harder for Inika, who had an additional weight of expectation to carry.

"I've been too scared to look at my phone all day, so it's been fine. I imagine once I do, I'll feel infinitely worse."

I pulled her in close, cuddling her tightly. Giving her that sense of strength and safety that alphas were meant to provide, though we so often failed at it.

"Sorry," Inika sighed. "This isn't what you came here for."

"I came here for you," I replied instantly. "This is fine, Inika. More than fine. Though, if you want to take the dress off and cuddle in your slutty corset, I'd also be on board with that."

Inika laughed, leaning back again, the ends of her hair tickling my hand. When she straightened, we were nearly nose-to-nose, and the temptation was too great to resist. Gently, so that she had plenty of time to move away, I gripped her chin, moving forward to brush my lips softly, experimentally against hers.

She chased me as I pulled back, grabbing my shoulders and holding on as she kissed me back. And then there was nothing soft or experimental about it.

The gentle nip of her teeth on my lower lip sent a shudder down my spine and all the blood in my body to my cock. The mood had shifted in an instant. Was it too much? Was I rushing her? It was hard to think when Inika was grinding her clit against the bulge in my jeans.

She pulled the dress out of the way for better friction, before yanking it off completely and dropping it on the floor.

"Princess..." I rumbled, an embarrassingly eager purr exploding out of my chest. "Look at you."

She flashed me a smug grin, clearly very pleased with the reaction she'd elicited. The corset was black and silky, pushing her breasts up high, practically begging for my mouth. In contrast, the knickers were a rough black lace, and she was practically riding the strip of fabric, slick seeping through it onto my jeans.

"You don't need to be gentle with me," Inika reminded me, digging her nails into my shoulders. "The cuddles were very sweet and appreciated, but you know I like the way we play."

"Remind me of your safe word."

"Audit," Inika replied patiently. She leaned in, pressing an almost sweet kiss to my lips before climbing off my lap and kneeling on the floor at my feet. My zipper was torturous, and I exhaled in relief as I pulled out down, releasing my dick from its prison.

"What do you want me to do, alpha?" Inika asked breathlessly, kneeling on the floor and staring up at me with wide, trusting eyes. That look made something twist sharply in my chest. It was so... precious. So fragile.

But she wanted me to fuck her, not coddle her, and I wasn't about to disappoint.

"Worship my cock, omega."

Inika melted into sub space instantly, shifting forwards until she was situated between my spread legs. I was already lazily fisting my shaft, my dick hard as steel. Shit. *Don't embarrass yourself.* Inika had been having a rough couple of days and I didn't want to add to that with a poor performance.

I removed my hand as Inika lifted herself up on her knees, nuzzling her cheek against my shaft. This was a bad idea. I was never going to last if she kept this up. She locked eyes with me as she licked from base to tip, swirling her tongue around the head and swiping up the precum that had been beading there. With a moan like she'd never tasted anything better in her life, she repeated the process, this time spending a little longer playing with the tip, massaging it with her tongue.

The entire time, her hands were never still. She rubbed my thighs, dug her nails into my abs, occasionally massaged my balls and the base of my knot. It could have been minutes or hours, I had no idea. It took me an embarrassingly long time to notice that she was edging me, when I'd been so confident that I was the one in charge here.

"Take off your knickers," I growled, gently lifting her off my cock by her hair.

Inika's lips were swollen, her eyes hazy as she looked up at me, shimmying out of her knickers while kneeling on the floor.

"Hold them up," I commanded before she could toss them aside. Inika's perfume grew impossibly thicker, her face burning with embarrassment as she held up the sodden scrap of lace. "How wet are they?"

"Wet," she rasped.

"You've barely checked, princess. You can do better than that. Put some effort in."

Inika glanced quickly at the fabric as she smoothed out the scrunched-up fabric, holding it up for me. "They're wet."

I tutted impatiently, making her perfume again. "Show me the gusset."

Inika whimpered as she turned over the fabric in her hand to show me the glistening crotch.

"Pass them here."

The sound she made was somewhere between a moan and a whine as she deposited the material into my hand.

"Now, this—" I rubbed the sticky gusset between my fingers, holding them up so she could see her slick shining on my skin. "Is more than just *wet*. These are ruined, aren't they? We need to get you some water, princess. You must be thirsty."

"I don't need water. I need cum."

"Greedy little slut," I replied affectionately. Inika's fingers were between her thighs before I'd even finished the sentence, eagerly playing with her clit. "Get on my lap and ride me."

Inika climbed onto the bed in an instant, her knees landing on either side of my thighs, slick dripping onto my cock as she lined herself up over me. Her perfect tits were in my face, and I pulled them over the top of the corset so I could worship each nipple in turn, firmly gripping each breast to hold her in place while she whined and tried to lower herself down on my cock.

"Patience," I chided, releasing her nipple with a pop. "How do you get any work done when you're panting after my cock all day, princess? It must be very distracting for you."

"You have no idea," Inika muttered, breaking character as she sank down on my dick, her eyes rolling to the back of her head.

She reached behind her, bracing her hands on my knees and rolling her hips, fucking me slowly and giving me the prettiest view I'd ever had in my life. Tits out, throat exposed, hair trailing down her back...

I memorised every inch of her.

"Are you putting on a show for me, omega?"

Inika nodded, letting out a rasping moan of pleasure as I circled her clit with my thumb.

"Cute." I pinched her clit lightly with my thumb and forefinger, and Inika arched her back instantly, trying to get closer. "Is that the best you can do, princess? Fuck me properly."

She was already a little cock drunk and sloppy as she clumsily grabbed my shoulders again, shifting her weight forwards for better leverage. Eventually, I'd bounce her on my dick and stuff her full of my knot, but not yet.

The anticipation made it all the sweeter.

"Blake," Inika whined, lifting herself up slowly before dropping back down onto my lap. "Help me."

"Those Pilates muscles hurting, princess?" I asked, kneading the back of her thighs.

She made a muffled sound of agreement, skin glowing with a fine sheen of sweat. "I need to come. I need your knot. *Please.*"

"Well, since you asked so nicely…"

I fell back on the bed, pulling her down with me before holding her up by her hips, thrusting up into her until I couldn't take it anymore, and rolling us.

Inika's dark hair fanned out around her head, a stark contrast against the white sheets. I hooked the back of her knees behind my forearms, pinning them up while I fucked her into the mattress, bumping her up the bed with each movement.

She circled her clit roughly with her fingers and that was it. The moment she clenched around me, I was done for, my knot swelling faster than it ever had in its life, like it was taking no chances about locking us together.

I moved my arms out of the way so she could lower her feet to the mattress, and she immediately unfastened the front clasps of the corset, letting it fall open to either side of her.

"That's not going to help this go down any faster," I muttered, keeping myself lifted on my forearms so I could admire the dips and curves of her body.

"Sorry," Inika replied serenely.

I snorted. "Minx."

She seemed surprised as I leaned down to kiss her, though she immediately reciprocated, her fingers finding that magical spot on my neck again.

Why hadn't I been kissing her this whole time? What was wrong with me?

Inika hummed contentedly, giving me a lazy smile as she flopped back onto the mattress. "I can't believe you made me hold up my knickers for you."

"Liked that, did you?"

"What does that say about me?" Inika mused. "No, don't answer that question."

"Yeah, let's not. I don't want to examine why I want to do the things I do to you."

"Well, a lid for every pot, as the saying goes," she shot back with a flirtatious smile.

I didn't even want to think about that. I couldn't let myself think that Inika was my perfect fit. If I did, I'd never let her go.

And if I kept her, I'd never make her happy.

Chapter 14

INIKA

Ugh.

I was so *sticky*.

There was still a week or so until my heat hit—I'd never been less prepared for it in my life—but the symptoms were really making themselves known this time around. It took all of the energy I had to crawl out of my nest and stumble into the bathroom, blasting the shower on lukewarm to cool myself off and scrubbing my sweat-soaked skin clean. Chances are tomorrow, I'd wake up feeling completely normal. This was just a little preview of the symptoms, but they wouldn't kick in properly for another few days.

I exhaled, pumping a liberal amount of Om-Guard body wash onto a washcloth. It was time to end the arrangement with Blake. It had to be. He—very reasonably—wasn't going to join me for my heat. I had to put some emotional distance between us now, especially if I was going to go ahead with an alpha-for-hire from Prendre.

Maia was drinking coffee in the kitchen, and I opted to join her there to eat breakfast, while Graeme huffed at the change in routine.

"So," Maia began, giving me a sidelong look. "Your parents *really* wanted to talk to you yesterday."

I grimaced. "Sorry. It didn't even occur to me that they'd be bothering you too."

She shrugged, unbothered. "I just kept repeating that I'd passed on their request for you to call them—which I did, though I don't think you read it—and left it at that."

"I avoided my phone yesterday. I might do the same today. I've got plenty of work to do—I'll just hole up in my office and only respond to company emails."

"Fair. You haven't really given me anything to do, but I have some Om-Guard stuff to work on if that's cool?"

"Of course." Technically, Maia was partially employed by the company too. Once upon a time, I'd really needed an assistant. My social calendar had been full, I'd hosted events, and served on boards and committees.

But perhaps I didn't really need one anymore? I wasn't doing any of that stuff and I had no intention of starting it again.

"Mmk. I might head into the office then if you don't need me. Mix it up a bit," Maia laughed, putting her cup in the dishwasher. "Have a good day."

"You too," I murmured. Graeme had already disappeared, possibly to go and unnecessarily supervise Blake who I'd heard arrive but hadn't seen as he'd bypassed the kitchen.

I ate my fruit and yoghurt alone in the cavernous room, feeling a little smaller than I usually did. Papa had chosen this house for me. It was around the corner from my parents and it had been purchased by the family trust, so it wasn't even technically *mine*. Not really.

Between the salary I'd been saving for years and the investments I had from the inheritance my grandparents had given me...

I *could* move. The idea had never occurred to me before. But why not? If I wasn't going to dedicate my future to being mated to the director of Om-Guard... Well, I didn't *have* to stay here.

Was this what a mid-life crisis looked like?

Or perhaps it was just my impending heat approaching and making me restless. Now probably wasn't the time to make any major decisions.

But I *was* tempted.

Shaking off the sudden urge to torpedo my entire life just for a change of scenery, I put my own dishes in the dishwasher and made two cups of tea in travel mugs. What I needed to be focusing on was the arrangements for my heat first. The existential crisis could wait until later.

I heard Blake before I saw him, his voice filled with frustration as he spoke to someone on the phone. He gestured for me to stay as I set the cup I'd made for him down on the scaffolding.

"Alright. I'll sort it out," he snapped before hanging up, exhaling heavily as he pocketed his phone. "Sorry. I didn't mean for you to hear that. Though I suppose I don't need to be quite so worried about professionalism with you," he added wryly, picking up his tea with a nodded thanks.

"Bit late for that," I agreed with a laugh. "Is everything okay?"

"Yes. Well, no." He frowned, surveying his surroundings. "I can't really leave now—I've already started plastering. But Freya's school is closed today and she needs picking up from a sleepover, but my brother is… out of commission. Dad was going to go, but the car has crapped out."

Blake shook his head, the frustration pouring off him in waves.

"I can get Freya? Or is that weird? It's probably weird." I shrugged. "But she's more than welcome to come and hang out with me here until you're finished for the day."

He paused with the cup halfway to his lips, giving me a considering look. "Are you sure? It's a bit of a trek to get there, but she wouldn't be a problem. Freya is very well-behaved."

"I know that." I gave him what I hoped was a reassuring smile. She was a great kid. "It's honestly fine. I've got a bunch of emails I need to answer. I'll do them in the car."

"If you're sure… I'll call the kid's mum and let her know to expect you."

"Perfect. Message me the address. I'll go rouse Lúcás." It was between him and Maia for who had the easiest job in the house these days. I barely went anywhere or did anything.

Traffic was awful, and it *was* a trek to Norbury, where Freya's friend lived, but the look on Freya's face made it entirely worth it. She threw open the front door with a beaming smile, barrelling down the path and throwing herself against me, her little arms wrapping tightly around my waist.

"Hi," I said gently, hugging her back, my heart turning into a puddle of goo in my chest. "How are you? Did you have fun with your friend?"

A beta woman came out of the house with a tentative smile, holding out a sparkly pink unicorn bag for me to take here. "Hi. Here are Freya's things—I think we got it all, didn't we, Freya? If not, Hallie can bring it to you at school. Sorry I couldn't drop her off—I've got six-month-old twins and leaving the house is a bit of a production these days."

"It was no trouble for me to pick her up," I assured her. The woman gave me a slightly bemused smile, glancing at the brand-new vehicle behind me with Lúcás sitting in the front seat. Admittedly, it did stand out a little. "Ready to go, Freya? You're going to come and hang out with me until your uncle finishes work. Is that okay?"

Freya squealed, releasing my waist only to grab my hand and drag me towards the car, shouting a hasty goodbye to her friend over her shoulder.

That she was so touchy-feely wasn't unusual—omegas were like that with people they cared about from the moment they could. I just hadn't expected to be part of that circle.

"What are we going to do at your house?" Freya asked, sliding across the backseat and buckling in. Shoot, did she need a car seat? Probably. I didn't know anything about children. "Oh hello, I'm Freya. What's your name?" she asked, noticing Lúcás in the driver's seat.

He grinned at her through the rearview mirror. "I'm Lúcás. How old are you, Freya?"

"Five and a half."

"I have a little boy that's just one year older than you," Lúcás replied.

I exhaled in relief at the proximity of an actual parent. "Do you usually sit in a car seat, Freya?"

She shrugged. "Not in Grandad's car. He says they didn't bother with them back in his day."

I caught Lúcás's lips twitch in the mirror. "There's a shop round the corner where we could probably pick up a booster."

"Let's do that then."

A booster seat and a smoothie later, we headed back to Mayfair, with Freya talking a mile a minute about the glitter slime she'd made at her friend's house.

Considering how unaccustomed I was to being around children—especially without another adult there as a buffer—it was a surprisingly easy experience. I suspected that Freya was so used to being around adults that she wholly expected to be spoken to like one anyway.

"This is your house?" she asked, flatting her nose to the window as the enormous double doors opened, allowing Lúcás to drive us directly into the courtyard.

"It is." I suddenly felt quite sheepish about it, imagining how large it looked from her perspective. Maybe I should call a realtor and just let the mid-life crisis run its course.

"Wow," Freya whispered. "It's like a castle."

"It is a bit," I agreed, my face heating as I caught Lúcás's eye in the rearview mirror.

Graeme met us in the courtyard as we climbed out of the vehicle, his mouth pressed into a thin line. Undoubtedly, Mama had already heard all about this. I was selfishly glad that her nervous temperament meant she wouldn't storm over here herself. She never went anywhere without Papa.

"This is a change in routine," he clipped. I could have sworn I felt my blood pressure rise in real time.

"It is," I agreed. "Come on, Freya. Let's go say hi to your uncle so he knows you got here safely."

She marvelled over everything as we headed up the stairs, trailing her fingers along the wall of windows in a way that I knew would deeply distress Graeme later. It wasn't the most kid-friendly of homes.

"There you are," Blake said, peering down at us from the scaffold above. "Everything alright?" he asked, looking at me.

"Fine," I assured him. "I thought we could go and make some lunch for all of us, Freya. What do you think?"

"Okay," she agreed instantly, bouncing on the balls of her feet.

"You don't have to do that," Blake said, still staring at me. "Frey can just camp out here and watch stuff on my phone. Don't feel like you need to entertain her."

"That's no fun—it's all dusty and noisy here. We can watch a movie on the big screen downstairs. It's really no hassle, Blake. I'll get some work done at the same time."

"Do you have a chef?" Freya asked once we were back in the kitchen. "Like at a real palace?"

"Sadly, no," I laughed. My parents employed a cook, but they entertained a lot more than I did. "But I quite like cooking. How about you?"

Freya climbed up onto one of the barstools, briefly making my heart stop in my chest until I was confident she wasn't going to tip over.

"Not really." She shrugged.

"I respect that. Do you eat prawns?"

She nodded, swinging her feet as I meandered around the kitchen, pulling out supplies. I'd asked Graeme to pick up the prawns with the vague idea of doing a prawn curry, but a risotto would be faster and easier, and it seemed more child-friendly.

What did kids even eat? I didn't own any chicken nuggets. I made a mental note that Graeme should add some of those to the grocery order next time. He'd love that.

I poured Freya a cup of water, setting it down in front of her on the island. Should I give her a snack while she waited for lunch? No, risotto didn't take long. I didn't want her to spoil her appetite.

That sounded responsible, right?

"Is Uncle Blake your boyfriend?" Freya asked nonchalantly as I started peeling and deveining the prawns, immediately making me fumble the one I was holding.

"Um, no." I laughed, though it sounded a little less natural than I'd hoped for.

"Why not?"

From the mouths of babes...

"We're just friends."

Freya pursed her lips, as though she was deciding whether she was going to start an argument or not.

"If you were Uncle Blake's girlfriend, you could be my aunty. I'd like that."

I was only human. How was I meant to stay detached in the face of that?

"That would be cool," I agreed. "But I get to be your friend instead, and that's pretty good too, right?"

Freya took a sip of her water, watching me over the rim of the cup. I wasn't sure I'd ever felt so judged in my life, and I'd had my fashion choices eviscerated in high-society magazines for years.

"I guess so. But I think it would be better if you were my aunty. I'll tell Uncle Blake that."

I suspected that I'd only make it worse if I tried to talk her out of it, so I changed the subject to her sleepover instead and hoped she'd forget all about it.

It was a quick meal to throw together, and half an hour later, Blake joined us around the island while I dished up bowls of pea and prawn risotto.

"Where's the butler?" he asked, looking around as though Graeme would pop out of a cupboard.

I did my best to hide my smile. "He has the afternoon off. I suspect he spends it having tea with Mama, though they're both very cagey about it when I ask."

Blake scowled at that, though he perked up considerably once he started eating.

"This is so yummy," Freya said. "Inika is a good cook, isn't she, Uncle Blake? I want her to be my aunty."

He went very red in the face, and I slid a glass of water across to him, shaking with laughter in my seat.

"However, Freya is happy that her and I are friends. Isn't that right, Freya?" I prompted.

"Kind of." She shrugged before shovelling an impressively large spoonful of risotto into her mouth.

"Great," Blake mumbled, clearing his throat. "I wonder what other interesting observations you'll come up with this afternoon, Frey."

She narrowed her eyes at him, understanding the sarcastic tone if not the actual words. Suddenly, she tilted her head, turning her gaze back on me in a way that was somewhat terrifying.

"Or you could be my dad's girlfriend—"

Blake made a strangled sound. "Don't even finish that sentence, Freya."

Chapter 15

BLAKE

"We're home!" Freya yelled, taking off her shoes and neatly stacking them on the rack by the door before turning around and watching to make sure I did the same. "Dad! Where are you?"

There was a muffled sound from the vague direction of Leo's bedroom and Freya skipped off, undoubtedly to fill him in on her afternoon at Inika's house. I had no idea what he'd make of it, but I was going to lose my shit if he complained so much as once. He'd known for months that Freya was going to have today off school, and he'd gone and got himself wrecked at that new club he'd found anyway.

He'd wanted to talk about it, but I'd avoided the conversation. I didn't want to indulge it anymore.

"Cup of tea?" Dad called from the kitchen.

"Please." I made my way down the hall, winding my way around baskets of laundry and assorted clutter. Freya was always going around after Dad and Leo, sorting their things into neatish piles, but my house had never looked like this before they'd moved in.

It felt selfish to even think it, considering what they'd been through, but I missed having my own space.

"Did you figure out what was wrong with the car?" I asked, entering the kitchen as Dad added a splash of milk to each cup.

"Blown head gasket. It's round at Jasper's now. He'll fix it." He was retired now, but Jasper had been a mechanic his whole life and had taken care of our vehicles for as far back as I could remember. "Hope it didn't leave you in too much of a lurch?"

Dad passed me the cup, looking sheepish.

I often wondered what Dad's reaction would have been if the roles between Leo and I were reversed. He'd always been harder on me than my twin. If I'd abandoned my parental duties whenever it was convenient or because I'd made stupid choices the night before, I doubted he'd have been as forgiving.

"Inika picked Freya up and looked after her for the afternoon."

Dad's eyes went wide. "That's awfully... generous of her."

"She's a very generous person."

"I know you don't want to talk about it, but I think I might have to ask anyway. What's going on here, Blake? This is no normal client relationship."

There was a large part of me that wanted to brush him off because that was the status quo. Whenever I'd needed to talk about something, Mum was the one I'd gone to. But she wasn't here anymore, and I'd lost touch with the few friends I'd once had because I hadn't put in any effort, and my twin was a fucking alien to me.

Shit, maybe I just wanted to talk about Inika. I wanted someone to know that this incredible, beautiful, interesting woman had for some reason chosen *me*, if only for a little while.

"We're friends." I cleared my throat. "And we're sleeping together."

"The friends part is probably more surprising than anything," Dad said drily. "It's pretty obvious that you've been sleeping with her. You've been far less miserable these past few weeks."

Had I?

"You're not getting attached though, are you?" Dad asked nervously. "You're from different worlds, son."

"I'm acutely aware of that."

Dad didn't look particularly reassured, and maybe it was because my tone wasn't as assertive as it could have been.

"I *am* aware of that," I reiterated. "I'm the one who said I couldn't commit when she asked me for more, um, time. Partly because I need to be here, but also because... well, I knew I wouldn't be able to do it without getting attached."

I'd left that part out when I was talking to Inika, mostly to preserve whatever shreds of dignity I had left.

Hey, thanks for asking me to casually fuck you senseless for five days solid but I might blurt out that I love you mid-orgasm and ruin the moment.

I blinked at the thought, quickly taking a gulp of my tea to hide whatever was happening on my face. Did I love Inika?

Probably not. Right?

I'd never been in love before, so I didn't have a frame of reference for it. But Inika didn't make me feel tortured or filled with longing or any of those things that the love songs said I was supposed to feel.

When I was around her, I just felt... content.

I didn't know what illness that was a symptom of.

"Did Leo leave his bed today?" I asked, desperate to change the subject.

Dad was suddenly very interested in the contents of his cup. "Go easy on him, would you? It's never been as easy for Leo as it was for you."

"We had the exact same upbringing," I pointed out scathingly. "We entered this world seven minutes apart."

It was exhausting, always treating Leo with kid gloves, never expecting him to take responsibility for his own actions. He had a kid of his own now. It was past time for him to grow up.

"I know, I know." Dad sighed, shifting his weight uncomfortably from one foot to the other. "Things just never came as easily to him as they did to you, Blake. You always did well in school, and you never worked particularly hard for it. You did well at sports. You excelled in the army, and picked up plastering like it was nothing, and manage the business side of it without much fuss. Leo has only ever been good with his fists, and you're not too shabby with those either."

"He managed to find himself a mate."

"He did," Dad agreed. "He found a mate and started a family, and it was the one time in his life where he felt like he'd beat you at something."

What a grim concept.

"I'm not in competition with Leo," I said firmly. "I never have been."

"I know. And I wish he wasn't in competition with you—I've told him so plenty of times over the years." Dad sighed heavily, setting his cup down on the counter with a thud. "For a while there, with Ella, he felt like he finally had it together. That he'd found a path that was purely his and he was going to walk it. That's not to say you've done anything wrong," he added hastily. "You taking him and Freya in has been a real lifesaver for them."

"Was it, though?" I asked quietly. "Or have I just enabled him? Because I can't help but wonder if living here has just been a convenient excuse for Leo to never get his shit together. But I'm not willing to gamble with Freya's health and happiness to find out."

Dad nodded, resigned. "You're a good son, Blake. A good uncle. A good brother, even when the chips are stacked against you. I'll talk to Leo again. We're putting too much of a burden on you, I can see that now. Your life has to be more than just us and work."

"I don't care about that," I lied. "I just want Leo to get it together for Freya's sake. That's all I'm worried about."

Blake: Is the car fixed?

Leo: Yup.

Blake: Can you drop off the wet-dry vac I left in the shed to the place I'm working on in Mayfair?

He didn't reply for several minutes, probably cursing me out for daring to make him get out of bed.

Leo: Fine. Send me the address.

I did, before instructing him to turn on his location so I could see with my own eyes that he was actually doing what I asked. Also, I wanted to intercept him out on the street. The last thing I needed was my bruised and beaten-up brother to show up on Inika's doorstep.

Honestly, she probably wouldn't care. If anything, she'd just be curious to meet Freya's dad. Graeme the butler might have a heart attack though, and I didn't need his death on my conscience.

Once I could see Leo moving closer on the map, I headed out through the staff entrance using my access card and crossed the quiet, elegant street to wait in front of the private green space that all these wanky houses have access to.

A sleek black car pulled up in front of the house that definitely *didn't* belong to my brother. I watched as a woman in a flashy-looking suit climbed out of the driver's seat, followed by three burly men who were too large to be anything but alphas.

They knocked on the door and were immediately ushered in by a blushing Graeme.

What the fuck was that about?

Leo rounded the corner in the rusty old beater that he and Dad shared, pulling up to the curb and winding down the passenger window. His face was still swollen and yellow with bruising. He looked a fucking state.

"Do you want this or not?" he asked loudly, gesturing at the vacuum and not bothering to turn down his music.

"Can you keep your voice down?" I hissed, opening the door to grab it before closing it again. "Try not to embarrass me in front of the client, will you?"

"What poncy asshole lives here?" he asked, squinting up at Inika's house. "Is this the place Freya was banging on about yesterday?"

"Yes. My *client* kindly helped with *your* childcare."

Leo scowled. "Well, it's not like I asked her to. Look after your own niece."

I had to walk away from this interaction before I burst a blood vessel.

"Come to that new club with me tonight," Leo called as I took a step away from the vehicle. "You'll like it. It's a way more interesting crowd than *Leviathan*. Deeper pockets. Fuck Ronnie anyway, right?"

"Sure, fuck Ronnie. But fuck you too, Leo. I'm not enabling your bullshit anymore. Every time you fight, you spend days recovering and sulking in bed. You're absolutely useless to Freya. Get your fucking life together, she doesn't need this shit."

He slammed down the accelerator so hard that I had to jump back before he ran over my foot, the prick. I rolled my shoulders, releasing the tension that came with every interaction with my brother recently. He'd get over it—by the time I got home, he'd probably be nagging me about going to that club again—but I was going to hold my ground this time.

I'd followed Dad's advice. I'd taken it easy on Leo. I'd given him the benefit of the doubt. It didn't seem to be working.

By the time I made my way back inside Inika's house, my source of frustration had shifted back to the three alphas who Graeme had ushered into the house. The soundproofing in this place was top-notch, but I hazarded a guess based on all the open doors I could see that they were in Inika's office. Was she alone in there with them except for the one beta woman they'd arrived with? For once, I hoped that Graeme was being a nosy prick and not giving Inika any space. He wasn't much, but he was *something*.

The rest of the day was an absolute write-off. As the clock ticked down to three pm, I got progressively less done, wondering what that meeting had been about.

Though not entirely wondering. I had my suspicions. And I didn't have any right to feel any kind of way about them.

By the time Inika made her way upstairs, I hadn't even showered yet. I was filthy, agitated, and in no state to fuck her the way she deserved. Yes, there was an element of degradation to how we played, but there was care behind it too. I couldn't give her the consideration that was needed when my head was like this.

"Oh," Inika said, coming to a halt as she rounded the corner, brow furrowing. "Did I get the time wrong?"

She looked so pretty in her forest-green shirt, loosely tucked into a short black skirt.

"No." I pushed my hands back through my hair, probably turning it grey with plaster dust.

Inika's body language changed right in front of my eyes. An omega responding to her alpha, soothing his distress, wanting to take own his emotional burden as her own.

Except I wasn't her alpha.

I could be her fuck buddy. I could be her friend. I could be the best damn plasterer she ever had. But her alpha? That was the one thing I could never be.

"I've been stressed this afternoon," I forced myself to say, using my words like a big boy. "Knowing those alphas were in your office. It made me... concerned for you."

Jealous, perhaps.

Maybe I wasn't using *all* of my words.

She exhaled heavily, giving me an apologetic look. "I'm doing my best to fight my instincts, but I think I'm going to have to give you a hug. I'm sorry."

"Don't be sorry," I said gruffly, catching Inika as she launched herself at me and hauling her up in my arms while she wrapped her legs around my waist.

It was terrifying, the way I immediately felt better. I pressed my nose to her throat, inhaling deeply for any trace of her natural scent beneath all the Om-Guard she slathered on each day.

If she wasn't leaning in, inhaling me like she'd die if she didn't, I'd be embarrassed that I was doing the exact same thing.

"Are you going to tell me who those alphas were?"

"You won't like the answer."

"They were from that heat agency thing, weren't they?" I sighed, having already known the answer deep down but not wanting to cop to it. I squeezed her a little tighter, trying not to let the unreasonable side of me win.

Inika had asked me to fulfil the role, and I said no. She'd made no promises about not finding someone else to do it, and frankly, it was wrong of me to even consider that she would.

Objectively, I was aware of that.

"And?" I growled. "Did you like any of them?"

"They seemed nice."

"You don't like nice."

She leaned back in my arms, looking down at me with one eyebrow raised. "Sometimes I like nice."

"Not during the sometimes when you'd need a knot-for-hire."

Inika narrowed her eyes at me, squeezing her thighs a little tighter around my waist. "Are you going to make this even harder, Blake?"

My hands found their way under her skirt, probably leaving dusty streaks on the globes of her ass. "I'm trying not to."

She exhaled heavily, her fingers clamping down on the back of my neck, making my eyes roll back.

Thank fuck none of the alphas she'd been interviewing had touched her. I didn't like to think how I'd react if I'd smelled their scent on her silky skin or expensive clothes.

In a vaguely homicidal way, probably.

"Who is the leading candidate?" I murmured. *What the fuck is wrong with you, Blake? You don't want to know the answer to that.*

"None of them were a good fit," Inika replied, the faintest hints of an omega purr distorting her words. My throat tightened at the realisation that she was soothing me, acting in the way that any nurturing omega would if an alpha she cared about was agitated.

Why was it so difficult to stay detached where Inika was concerned? It wasn't like she was *trying* to make me like her. She'd asked me to fill the role of a knot-for-hire for her heat. Inika was sticking to our "it's just sex" agreement better than I was.

No, she wasn't *trying* to make me like her, but I liked her anyway. Just for who she was—her filthy kinks, her sharp wit, how kind she was with Freya—the whole package.

Fuck me, I was in trouble.

My hands tightened a little on her ass, squeezing her more possessively than I had any right to.

"Something you want, alpha?" Inika asked in a low, seductive voice that seemed to travel down my spine and work its way around to my knot.

Did she know that my cock ached every time she called me that?

But I didn't tell her that. Instead, I tutted disinterestedly, because that was what Inika wanted from me, and I'd already strayed too far from the bounds of what this was. From all that it could be.

"Something *I* want? You're the one climbing all over me with your ass hanging out, omega."

She let out a little whimper of need, pressing herself against my front, scentmarking me in a way that had the tension I'd been holding since I'd seen those alphas finally releasing.

"Fuck me. Use me. Please, Blake."

"Oh, I will definitely be using you, princess. But fucking you? Giving *you* pleasure?" I snorted. "You can wait. First, I need to shower."

Inika slid down my front, grabbing my hands and tugging me down the hallway.

Away from the spare room.

"Inika…"

"Let me have this," she murmured. "I want my nest to smell like you. Just for a little while."

"We both know this is a bad idea."

"I enjoy making bad decisions with you."

I couldn't argue with that logic.

Most nest doors *looked* out of place in the rest of the home. They were retrofitted once the technology had been invented to make a nest more secure during heats. Unsurprisingly, Inika's was so state-of-the-art that the door looked entirely in keeping with the rest of the house.

She rested her hand on the handle for a long moment, and there was a faint buzz before it gently beeped, recognising the handprint and releasing the locks.

Inika's room wasn't at all what I expected it to be. Given that she always dressed in neutral, muted colours, I was surprised to find that her nest was an explosion of colour. The nest was a raised platform, just a few inches above the floor, and it was covered in deep, jewel-toned cushions and blankets in every material I could imagine.

There was sleek, built-in storage around the walls, but I had no doubt that there was a separate walk-in wardrobe within this suite of rooms for her clothes.

"Come wash up in here," Inika said, pulling me into her en suite. The rich colour palette continued into this room too, with Victorian-green gloss tiles on the walls, a traditional black-and-white pattern on the floors, and trailing plants on every surface.

Was *this* Inika's style? Nothing else in the house looked like this.

I shucked my dirty clothes while Inika fiddled with the knobs on the wall, turning on the rainfall showerhead. The moment the water was warm, I moved under the spray, scrubbing myself clean.

Inika stood outside the walk-in shower, peeling off her own clothes, a hungry look in her eyes as she watched me.

"Turn around," I ordered. She twirled slowly, and I admired the dusty handprints I'd left on her golden-brown skin.

"Am I dirty?"

"Filthy," I purred, grabbing her hand and tugging her into the stall but not all the way under the water, careful not to get her hair or make-up wet.

"Hands on the wall, ass out, omega."

Inika's hands hit the wall with an echoing slap that had me pausing for a moment, worried she'd injured herself.

No, she was fine. Just eager.

I gently tugged her head back so she was looking at me upside down.

"Look at you," I sighed in mock disappointment. "Cock drunk already. You make this embarrassingly easy."

"Sorry, alpha."

"No, you're not."

Inika's smile turned wicked. "No, I'm not."

With another put-upon sigh, I released her, pumping soap into my hands so I could massage the handprints off her ass. Unfortunately, her entire bathroom was basically an Om-Guard product catalogue, but any scent I washed away with the soap I'd soon have back again once I got her perfuming.

The moment she was clean, I dropped to my knees behind her, roughly grabbing her cheeks and licking her dripping cunt from behind.

"Blake!" Inika shrieked, her hand slapping the wet tile again while she pressed her pussy back against my face. "Oh my... Yes. Keep doing that."

Her slick soaked my chin as she came, and it would have been easy to wash it off but I didn't want to. I wanted to wear her scent on my skin like a badge of honour.

"Nest," Inika rasped, fumbling for the shower lever and slamming it down.

"Are you sure about this?"

"Very."

She threw me a towel, hastily drying herself off before grabbing my hand and tugging me back towards her room.

I hadn't noticed it when we'd come in, but from this angle, there was very clearly something buried in the nest that wasn't a jewel-coloured cushion or linen sheet.

Inika let out a muffled squeak as I pushed a cushion aside to pick it up.

"What's this?" I asked, casually turning the electric-blue dildo over in my hands and making a show of examining the suction base.

"Dildo," Inika mumbled, the perfume of her desire loudly making its presence known.

"Speak up, princess. I can't hear you."

She cleared her throat. "It's a dildo."

"Is it now?" I hummed, wrapping my hand around the thick base, my middle and thumb barely touching. I raised an eyebrow at Inika, enjoying the way her thighs clenched. "This is very thick, Inika. Is your cunt really so greedy?"

She bit down on a faint moan, dark eyes taking on that hazy, needy look they had when she needed a good fucking.

"Yes."

"Interesting. What about your greedy throat, hm? Can you take it?"

She nodded, standing up on wobbly legs and taking the thick toy from my hands. Like the good girl she was, Inika immediately lifted it to her lips.

I sighed heavily, shaking my head. "It has a suction base, Inika."

She blinked at me before lowering herself to her knees, cheeks flushed and a trail of slick running down her inner thigh as she glanced at the hardwood floor. She looked up at me for approval and I shook my head again.

"Where...?" Inika asked hesitantly, glancing around the room.

"The mirror."

She closed her eyes for a moment, breathing heavily. It did spectacular things to her breasts.

"Need your safe word?" I asked casually, quickly adjusting myself while she wasn't looking.

"No," Inika rasped.

"Then get up, stick that dildo on the mirror, and watch yourself deep throat it, wishing it was my cock."

She whimpered as she climbed to her feet and headed for the ostentatious gilt mirror that hung on the wall.

I came to stand behind her as Inika pressed the suction base to the glass, wanting to make sure she could see me watching her work in the reflection. It made for quite the contrast—the antifreeze-coloured dildo, complete with veins, on the antique Baroque mirror, decorated with golden cherubs and grapes on the vine.

Inika glanced at me in the mirror, her face flushed and eyes hectic as if I'd already fucked her into several orgasms, but it was just her *brain* making her feel this way. God, she was incredible. A sexually confident, bold, and beautifully submissive miracle.

"Suck, Inika."

Without hesitation, she opened her mouth and wrapped those pouty lips I spent far too much time thinking about around the bulbous silicone cockhead.

"Don't look at me," I growled, my body stiff with tension from the effort of staying in place. "Watch yourself. See how deep you can take it."

<h1 style="text-align:center">Chapter 16</h1>

INIKA

I was going to be kneeling in a puddle at this rate.

My eyes watered. Drool leaked out of the corners of my mouth. And my pussy was a full-blown waterfall.

Every time I bobbed my head, taking the silicone further down my throat, it filled the room with the lewdest squelching, gagging sound I'd ever made in my life. My face burned with a desperate kind of humiliation, and it made me *ache* for the stretch of Blake's knot.

I was being a good girl. I wanted my reward.

Blake squeezed his shaft and I released the dildo immediately, letting out an omega growl of discontent. That was mine. I wanted it.

"In the nest, omega," he said lazily, a smug grin on his face as he helped me up.

He didn't need to tell me twice. I kept hold of his hand, dragging him with me.

"Wait," I ordered, climbing onto the mattress and organising things the way I wanted them so there was a perfect, Blake-sized spot in the middle. "Okay. Now, come in."

That it was the first time I'd ever had an alpha—or *anyone*—in my own personal nest didn't register until much later. In the moment, all I cared about was getting on that sweet, sweet knot and orgasming until I forgot my own name.

Hadn't I meant to end this arrangement yesterday?

Best not think about that now.

Blake was ever the conscientious alpha, letting me shift him where I wanted him and arranging cushions around him once I had him in place. For a long moment, I just admired him lying there amongst my things, increasingly drenched in my scent.

What a pretty picture he made.

"You finished staring, princess?"

"I don't know. You're very easy to stare at."

I could have sworn he blushed this time.

Instead of waiting for him to take the lead, I shuffled down the bed on my knees, straddling one of Blake's legs and bending over him to take his cock into my mouth.

In the back of my mind, I was faintly aware of the warning bells telling me that this *had* to be the last time. My heat was approaching. The hallway project was nearly done. I was going to have to deal with the fallout with my friends and family.

All of the walls were closing in on me at once. But for now, I was in paradise and I planned on enjoying every second of it.

"Omega..." Blake rasped, arching back and bucking his hips as I took him deeper, moaning at the taste of his precum on my tongue.

He wasn't mine, but he tasted like he was.

"Up," Blake snarled, all impatient alpha as he tugged my head up, easily lifting me up his body and sitting me on his cock. I sunk down with a half moan, half gasp of surprise, my eyes rolling back into my head.

Oh, how I was going to miss this.

Between the mirror show and the blow job, I'd pushed Blake to breaking point. There was no dirty talk now, just ragged sounds of pleasure as he moved my body, using me exactly the way I wanted to be used.

Like I was just an omega fucktoy, there for his pleasure.

I came almost instantly, clenching around him as Blake continued to bounce me on his cock. My nails dug into his chest, desperately attempting to keep myself upright, though nothing had ever felt harder.

"Fuck, princess," Blake rasped, veins and tendons standing out in stark relief as he held back his own orgasm. "Tell me this pussy is mine."

This was a dangerous game. And yet...

"It's yours. This pussy is yours."

I didn't think it was possible for me to get any wetter, but that did it. Blake's hands were possessive everywhere they touched me, his fingertips feeling like brands against my skin.

As much as I wanted to drag this moment out—because we couldn't keep doing this, we *couldn't*—my body wasn't cooperating with my demands to make this last.

This time, I took him over the edge with me. My wobbly arms gave out, but Blake caught me before I could collapse, guiding me down so that I was laying on his chest, my nose at his throat.

It was *such* a position of trust, and combined with the fact that we were in my nest—a space I'd never shared with anyone—it sort of made me want to cry.

What an unsexy impulse. I deliberately clenched around Blake's knot, the ripple of sensation setting off another wave of orgasms that distracted me from everything else that was going on. Everything I couldn't have, everything I needed to do, everything that was out of my control.

There was no problem that an orgasm couldn't fix. At least for a few minutes.

Blake's fingers found the base of my spine, but instead of stroking it like he usually did, he began probing gently at the muscle.

"You're so tense," he murmured, rubbing a spot that I hadn't even realised was stiff until he'd started massaging it.

My eyes drifted shut, and I all but melted against him as he worked his way up my back, the occasional rumble of a purr breaking free before he quickly got it under control again.

Had this been a terrible idea? My nest reeked of him—of us—in the best possible way, but it was going to be torture to sleep in it tonight. I'd never be able to look at the tiles in my shower again without remembering how it felt to be pushed up against them, with Blake's tongue buried in my pussy from behind.

I might genuinely have to burn both the mirror and the blue dildo currently suctioned on to it.

What was it about Blake? I couldn't seem to stop making bad decisions where he was concerned. The last time I'd been this willing to make questionable life choices where an alpha was concerned was when I'd fallen in love with a Spanish waiter on a whirlwind holiday when I was nineteen, only to be ghosted the day after I'd flown home.

Mama had been quite adamant afterwards that I hadn't been in love with him—that I'd imagined the whole thing—but I'd never been so sure about that. Love wasn't a finite resource. It may not always be logical, and it may not always be forever, but there was plenty of it to go around.

In my own incredibly immature and naive way, I'd loved Marco.

But I was *in love* with Blake, and that was a far more terrifying prospect.

I was in love with the way he treated me. The way he treated Freya. I was in love with his integrity, his drive, his discipline.

I was in love with Blake, and it was probably going to ruin my life.

I dived into the shower the moment Blake's knot had gone down, and by the time I emerged wrapped in a towel, he'd left. Which wasn't surprising, and wasn't even a bad thing because what would I have done if he was still there?

And yet, it stung a little, regardless.

Shaking it off, I pulled out a plum-coloured loungewear set, fully intent on spending the evening in my inconveniently perfect-smelling nest, watching the most mindless movie I could find. Maybe I'd order a greasy pizza. It was my favourite indulgence, especially right before and right after my heat.

The intercom beeped gently on the wall, disturbing the peace I was desperately trying to acquire. But Graeme only buzzed directly into the nest if it was urgent, so I padded across the room to answer him.

"Um, Ms Dara?" he began uncomfortably. "Your father is here to see you."

I took a deep breath in, using Blake's lingering scent to calm myself, before exhaling.

"I'll be right down. We'll take tea in the drawing room—"

"Your father felt the dining room would be more appropriate."

And, of course, Graeme had agreed without hesitation despite the fact that this was my house and I theoretically set the rules.

I disconnected the conversation without saying goodbye, scraping my hair back into a neat ponytail, slipping my feet into slides, and dousing myself with Om-Guard from head to toe.

It had probably been close to twenty years since my father had seen me without a stitch of make-up on, dressed in lounge clothes. I'd spent my evenings when I was away at school looking like this, but I was expected to put my best foot forward on weekend visits to my parents.

Graeme would have mentioned if Mama was here, so at least I didn't have to deal with the fallout from her seeing my outfit. She'd have probably fainted, and it would have turned into a whole thing.

I startled at the sound of tools clinking together further down the hall as I headed out of my nest and downstairs. Blake had apparently left my nest, but he hadn't actually left the house yet. Maybe he was just packing up for the day.

"Inie," Papa said, looking at me in surprise as I entered the dining room where he was already sitting at the head of the table. "Did I wake you?"

"No." I took the seat kitty-corner to him, choosing not to elaborate.

"Inie," Papa sighed. "We really must talk about that... *conflict* the other morning. You've been avoiding us—Mama is very worried, you know. It's very unkind of you to do this to her."

I squeezed my fingers together in my lap, digging my nails into the backs of my hands to stop myself from saying something that I'd regret later, like "I'm sorry. I'll be a good omega. Please stop being mad at me. It makes me want to crawl out of my own skin."

Those were instincts talking, though. And I was more than just my instincts.

"I'm going to buy my own house after this heat has passed," I said calmly. "With my own money. You can have this one back."

Not that it had ever been in my name or anything to begin with.

"Honestly, this is a decision I should have made a long time ago. I supposed, with Om-Guard always on the table and yet not quite in my reach, I felt as though I *couldn't* make a decision yet. But now we have clarity over that situation—"

"We do *not*," Papa insisted.

"—I'm able to make plans of my own with a clear conscience. Inika Dara has always felt like a role I had to play. I want to find out who I am when... well, when no one else is watching, I suppose."

I thought of Blake and the way he looked at me—both in bed and out of it—and admitted to myself that perhaps that statement wasn't entirely true. I *liked* who I was when *he* was watching.

When all was said and done, I really hoped we could at least stay friends.

"This isn't like you, Inie," Papa fretted, shaking his head. "Your heat is approaching, and you've been alone so long. It's making you think crazy things."

"A lot of thought has gone into this over a number of years, Papa. Please don't reduce all of that down to heat hormones, it's incredibly disrespectful."

"It's the only thing it can be," he insisted. "I will ask Dr Batuk to come out and visit you—"

"I don't need to see a doctor."

"—she always has excellent advice." Papa nodded to himself, satisfied that he'd solved the problem. Typical alpha nonsense. They barged in without a shred of situational awareness, did whatever they wanted without consultation or feedback, and declared the problem solved.

I thought about arguing with him, but there wasn't any point. He'd send Dr Batuk around, regardless. At the very worst, I could have a general physical done.

"I will arrange that for you," Papa said decisively, pushing out of his seat and already heading for the door. "All will be well. She will give you whatever it is you need. And then we can discuss this Hugo again, yes? Yes. All will be as it should be."

I sighed heavily, pouring myself a cup of tea from the untouched tray on the table and adding a dash of milk before carrying it upstairs with me in the hopes that it would help me settle down.

Papa had got so in my head that for a brief moment, I'd forgotten that Blake was still upstairs in the hallway. While soundproofing had been added to most of the house, the dining room had enormous archways on three sides, opening it up to the other rooms for entertainment purposes. There was no soundproofing *that*.

"Everything okay?" Blake asked, looking at me like he already knew the answer.

"Fine," I replied quickly, following it up with my best attempt at an airy laugh. "Just my parents being... overbearing. I'm practically geriatric for an unmated omega. I'm sure I don't have to explain to you how that goes."

He probably hadn't had *quite* the same pressure put on him, but mating and settling down was still very much seen as the only acceptable path for alphas and omegas, despite all the empowering self-determination talk we'd parroted at school.

Blake watched my expression closely. "Not really. Once Leo took a mate, my parents never really brought up the subject with me again. Apparently, so long as they got at least *one* grandkid, they were content to leave the subject alone. Though, maybe if Ella hadn't died and then Mum shortly after, they'd have expected me to settle down." He shrugged. "There's no way of knowing now."

Guilt churned uncomfortably in my stomach. Blake had real problems. Heavy problems, like grief and the challenges of raising a child who'd lost her mother. And I suspected that he didn't whine half as much as I did.

"Well," I began awkwardly, sidestepping him so I could return to the safety of my nest. "I'll see you tomorrow, I guess. Sorry you had to hear... all of that."

Blake scowled. "Don't apologise for that. Are you sure you're okay?"

"Positive."

Not even a little.

Chapter 17

BLAKE

"Can you walk me to school today, Uncle Blake?" Freya asked, wandering into the kitchen in her pyjamas as I sat at the table drinking my coffee.

I glanced at the time on the microwave. Usually, I struggled to do the school run with my work hours, but today was pack down day and the scaffolding crew wouldn't be at Inika's until ten. Probably eleven, knowing Jordy. He was always late.

"Sure, Frey." I took my coffee with me as I headed over to the bench to make her breakfast.

"Good." She climbed into the seat I'd just vacated. "Grandad got so tired yesterday that we had to stop lots on our walk, and then I was late."

I paused, milk bottle hovering over the cereal bowl. "He was getting tired?"

"Mmhm, from walking. Grandad says he's too old to be traipsing around town."

That definitely sounded like something Dad would say. My stomach churned with guilt. He'd have had to walk home after dropping her off too. How many stops had he made out of exhaustion on the way back? Was he ever going to tell us about it? Probably not. It would be just like him to suffer in silence.

I set Freya up with her breakfast before heading upstairs, knocking on Dad's door and quietly letting him know that he could sleep in and I'd get Freya off to school. I didn't even bother letting Leo know. If he wanted to know where his daughter was, he could try fucking parenting her for a change.

Freya went off to school easily, and I jogged back home before climbing in the van and heading straight to Inika's house, stuck in traffic most of the way.

Graeme ignored me as I passed him in the corridor, heading upstairs.

Before Jordy and his crew arrived, I made sure the scaffolds were clear of my own stuff, before doing my initial clean of the floor, loading up the van with any big pieces of plaster and doing a round with the hoover.

I was done. The job was finished. In all honesty, it could have been done a couple of days ago, but I'd been dragging the process out.

Enough was enough, though. If we let this go on any longer, we were only going to end up hurting each other's feelings. Inika's approaching heat was a deadline we couldn't negotiate with.

Not only that, but this morning had proven that I needed to be spending more time at home. Maybe I could bring on an apprentice. I'd put it off, assuming that Leo would eventually be less useless, but clearly that had been overly optimistic of me.

I stood aside as the scaffolding crew removed their gear, packing up my tools as I went, ready to load them in the van.

Where was Inika? While she used so much Om-Guard that it was impossible to track her scent around the house anyway, I usually had some vague idea of where she was, if only based on how the rest of the staff were acting. But everyone was quiet today, and I wondered if Inika had even emerged from her nest this morning.

Fuck, I wanted to check on her so bad. I wanted to crawl into that jewel-coloured nest with her, and tell her that her dad was a prick—the words I'd wanted to say yesterday, but had chickened out of saying.

He was, though.

The problem was, I was too.

Who the fuck was I to complain about how other people treated Inika when I literally got off on degrading her? Yeah, she got off on it too, but I still felt like I was in no position to defend her honour.

Once the guys were done, I removed the protective floor covering and hoovered up every bit of dust I could reach. Undoubtedly, Graeme would be along afterwards to polish, tutting and complaining, but he didn't have anything to complain about.

It looked fucking phenomenal in here.

The rest of the house was still boring—with the exception of Inika's suite of private rooms—but the ceiling above this formerly abandoned staircase was a fucking masterpiece once more.

Inika appeared right as I was considering messaging her, dressed surprisingly casually in loose forest-green shorts and a matching top that hung off one shoulder. She'd pulled her hair up off her neck, though loose strands curled around her face, and I was pretty sure she didn't have any make-up on.

It took everything in me not to snatch her up into my arms and carry her away to whatever nest she'd let me into, just to hold her.

"Blake..." Inika breathed, staring up at the ceiling. "It looks *incredible.* I love it."

"I'm glad," I grunted, forever uncomfortable with anyone complimenting my work.

She looked up at me with a beaming smile, eyes shining with happiness, and my lungs were suddenly too small to hold the air I needed.

"We have to stop doing this now," I rasped, my throat strangely tight. "This... Us. We need to stop."

Her expression shuttered right in front of my eyes, all of that openness melting into perfect... politeness.

I felt my heart crack in my chest.

"You're probably right." She exhaled like the weight of the world was on her shoulders, and all I wanted to do was take it away. "I've honestly been thinking the same—I'm not just saying that to assuage my ego. I'm not confident that I had the courage to make the call, and it's... Well, it's time."

"What do you mean by that?" I asked, my throat dry. "What do you mean you didn't have the courage to make the call? I never want you to feel afraid around me, Inika."

"I'm not afraid," she assured me with a brave smile, though her eyes were sad. "Never that. I've just grown more attached to you than is probably appropriate, considering the circumstances. That's my responsibility to manage, not yours," she added hastily when I opened my mouth. "And I'm sure it'll pass with time as these things do. I certainly hope you'll still feel that you can call on me as a friend and support system for Freya. I really would like to keep in touch with her."

I nodded mutely, not trusting myself to speak. If "I've grown attached" had felt like a spear to the gut, it was nothing compared to "it'll pass."

Those two words had unravelled my entire world.

With one last sad smile, Inika backed away, her gaze lingering on my face until the last possible moment. And then she rounded the corner and she was gone, leaving me alone in the hallway.

Had she gone back to her nest? Did it still smell like me? If it did, she was probably stripping off the linens right now.

That thought had no right to hurt as much as it did.

This had always been a dangerous game. It was always going to feel like paradise at the time, and an acute kind of agony when it ended.

The ventilation system kicked into overdrive as I gathered up the last of my things, cycling fresh air through the corridor and erasing the last of my scent.

With shaking hands, I headed down through the staff entrance and out to my van, leaving my access card on the kitchen counter on my way past.

It'll pass.

Maybe it would for Inika. She wanted love, she wanted a mate, she just hadn't found the right one yet. When she did—and how could she not? Inika was perfect—she'd remember me as a fond blip in her memories.

I'd remember her as my one great love.

Chapter 18

INIKA

Well, getting up this morning had been a mistake.

I'd known it was going to be. I'd put it off as long as possible, hiding in my nest with my laptop to get some work done and refusing to acknowledge the outside world.

It had already gone pear-shaped with Papa's visit yesterday, but it wasn't until later that night, when I'd wandered over to Blake's worksite, that things had started feeling really bleak.

He'd never mentioned that the job was done. When I checked the calendar that Graeme kept in the kitchen, I noted that the scaffolders were coming back today to pack down, so clearly he'd known that this was the final day he'd be here.

Embarrassingly, I'd read something into it. My idiot brain had thought that he wasn't making a big deal about the fact that the job was done because he still wanted to see me in some capacity.

And why had I thought that? He'd never given me any reason to.

I'd let myself get carried away when I'd invited Blake to my nest yesterday. That had been a stupid decision.

I didn't regret it, but it had been a stupid decision.

The bedding, still saturated with our combined scent, seemed to beckon me in, and I stripped out of my clothes as fast as possible so I could burrow against the fabric with my bare skin.

Was I going to cry?

I didn't want to. Intellectually, I found the idea of crying over men to be an unappealing prospect. But emotionally, maybe a good sob would make me feel more at peace.

In the end, the tears didn't come. I was tired, and hollow, and uncomfortable though I was struggling to pinpoint exactly why. Saying goodbye to Blake had made everything feel wrong, and I welcomed the sweet reprieve that sleep provided, just for the break from my thoughts.

By the time I woke up, it was clear that heartbreak wasn't my only affliction. Maybe it was because of how attached I'd got to Blake, or that I'd coated my nest in his scent as though he was my alpha, but something had kicked my heat off early.

Shit.

I didn't have time for this. I wasn't ready.

Dragging myself out of my nest, I pulled on the same co-ord set I'd been wearing earlier and forced myself to leave my rooms. I needed a big, protein-heavy meal now to sustain me for the next five days or I was going to be miserable.

"Inika," Maia gasped as I came into the kitchen, taking a step towards me before seeming to think better of it and giving me space. Or perhaps I'd snarled at her. I wasn't feeling entirely in control of my responses. "Are you okay? Should I call someone?"

"I need to eat," I mumbled, stumbling towards the fridge.

"Here, I made a huge pot of bolognese. I'll get you a bowl. Sit, sit. Graeme has clocked off for the day, shall I call him back?"

I shook my head. Graeme was the last person I wanted to see.

"Let the office know," I instructed before thanking her for the giant bowl of spaghetti she slid in front of me. "I'm going to be unavailable from tomorrow."

She nodded, already pulling out her phone. "And what about that agency? Should I call them?"

I shoved a forkful of pasta into my mouth to put off answering. I'd never chosen a candidate. They'd suggested another round of interviews and I'd put it off, having struggled so much with it the first time.

"No," I replied eventually. "I'll get through without them."

Maia chewed on her lower lip, phone still raised in front of her. "Have you ever before?"

"Not since my first heat." I grimaced at the memory. As much as I didn't want to admit what a delicate little flower I was, I had a very low tolerance for discomfort. "I'll survive."

Maia drummed her nails on the back of her phone case. "Is this because of the plasterer?"

I looked up sharply, and Maia shot me an apologetic look. "Sorry, I don't mean to pry. It's just that, well, Graeme kept complaining about him and it was obvious—though only to me apparently—that you were, you know, sleeping with the guy. No judgement," she added hastily. "Get it, girl."

"He's not my alpha," I said, though I wasn't sure whose benefit I was saying it for. Perhaps I was just reminding myself. "Just call work. I'll handle the rest."

I breathed through a sudden cramp, pushing the half-eaten bowl of pasta away. The loose cotton top and shorts that I was wearing felt too heavy considering how hot my skin was, but I couldn't realistically strip off any more layers.

"Take my phone," I said, pulling it out of my pocket and shoving it towards Maia. "Don't give it back to me until my heat passes, no matter how much I beg."

She nodded, immediately hiding the device from view. It was a miracle I hadn't sent a desperate message to Blake already, and my self-control was only going to get weaker from here.

A burning tear tracked over my overheated face, and everything was so uncomfortable that I wanted to claw my own skin off my body for relief.

This time, I couldn't quite suppress my pained whine. I didn't want a service alpha. I wanted *my* alpha.

Why didn't he want me? How was I meant to survive this without him?

A valiant little voice in the back of my head tried to remind me that I did this all the time. Not alone, granted, but I *could* and *would* survive a heat by myself. That I'd survived without an alpha to call my own all of these years, and I'd keep managing it until I found the alpha who was truly meant to be mine.

But that voice was fighting an uphill battle. All I wanted right now was Blake.

Chapter 19

BLAKE

"You two are great company this evening," Dad groused, glaring at me then Leo in turn.

Leo looked up from his phone, face still a medley of colours from an assortment of bruises, seemingly surprised that there was anything amiss.

"What's your problem?" he asked me gruffly.

"I don't have a problem," I shot back, briefly contemplating suggesting that we go to that new club Leo had found. This time, I was the one with some aggression I needed to work out. It wouldn't help, though.

It might in the moment, but ultimately, I'd just end up feeling worse.

We all started as my phone buzzed, lighting up offensively where I'd abandoned it on the arm of the chair.

Unknown Number.

"Who's calling you?" Leo asked at the same time Dad said, "Bit late for a client to be calling, isn't it?"

"Hello?" I said, holding the phone up to my ear and ignoring both of them.

"*Hi. Is this Blake Alwis?*" a nervous, feminine voice replied.

"It is."

"*This is Maia Gallagher. Inika's assistant.*"

Fuck. I stood immediately, ready to... I wasn't sure what. Something. Anything. Whatever was required.

"What's going on? Is Inika okay?"

"*Yes and no.*" Maia cleared her throat. "*Her heat seems to have come early. Possibly from being involved with an alpha in the lead-up,*" she added, and I absolutely heard the censure in her voice.

"I can't..." I exhaled heavily, fingers flexing at my side. I wanted nothing more than to go to her. At the same time, I selfishly wished that Maia hadn't told me what was going on. Ignorance was bliss, and now I had to think about Inika in heat and I doubted I'd be able to think about anything else. "She asked me if I could go into her nest and I already explained that I couldn't. Have you called that... agency?" I asked, forcing the word out.

"*Inika told me not to. She only wants you. But she's also respectful of the fact that you said no, and gave me her phone with strict instructions not to let her have it back until her heat is over. Look, I shouldn't be calling you at all, but I don't know... I had to check. I had to try. She's in pain, and she's going through it alone. I know this is normal for omegas or whatever, but I've never seen it before and it looks fucking horrible.*"

Maia had been a fucking pain to deal with when she was hunting me down to work on Inika's house, but I was suddenly very grateful that she had such a compassionate assistant.

"I can't—" Leo snatched the phone out of my hand before I could finish my sentence, holding it to his ear and shoving me back when I went to grab it.

"Let me talk some sense into him. He'll call you right back," he said before hanging up and tossing my phone to Dad, who clumsily caught it and shoved it underneath him on the seat.

"Very mature," I snarled.

"What's going on?" Leo demanded, crossing his arms over his chest. "Who asked you into her nest? Does someone want you as a mate?"

"You never said she'd invited you into her nest," Dad said accusingly.

Leo looked between us. "*Who*? Who is this omega?"

It felt a little jarring to be on this side of the interrogation.

"His client," Dad supplied. "Inika Dara. Jasper's heard of her, you know. The Om-Guard heiress."

Leo's eyes went wide. "Bit out of your league, isn't she?"

"Obviously," I snapped. "She wasn't asking me to be her mate. She was asking me to service her through her heat."

Dad and Leo exchanged looks like they were debating which one of them would have to give me the birds and the bees talk again.

"I know that usually ends in a mating bite," I added, exasperated. "I may not have ever had a mate, but I do understand how it works. It's different for rich people. There are services they can hire. Alphas they can borrow for heats."

Dad choked on the sip of beer he'd just taken. "How does that work then?"

"Do we need to talk about this?" I groused. "There are muzzles involved. And a support crew outside the nest. Birth control shots. Probably a bunch of other stuff that I'm forgetting."

"And your client just asked you out of nowhere to be her knot-for-hire?" Leo asked in disbelief.

"Well, he was already shagging her."

I glared at Dad. "Thanks for that."

"I just don't really get what you're doing here then," Leo sighed. "You must have liked her enough for that—"

"I like her a lot more than that."

"—and if you can use these muzzle things, you're not going to commit to a mating you're not ready for."

"Which is wise," Dad added. "I want you to find a mate, Blake. But it's not a decision that should be entered into lightly, and you haven't known this bird very long."

"Right," Leo agreed. "So he could just spend this heat with her—which I'm sure she'd appreciate, poor thing must be miserable—and then date her afterwards. And then maybe go into her next heat muzzle-free. Or breakup if it doesn't work out. What's the problem here?"

"What the fuck are you talking about?" I snarled. "I can't just up and leave for five days. I've got responsibilities here. And what would I do with a mate? What have I got to offer her? What kind of life would I provide an omega—let alone one like Inika?"

"A great life," Dad replied, affronted. "A little unconventional, sure. But omegas are generally very sociable—that you're close with your family probably wouldn't be a deal breaker for the vast majority of them. You've got a good career. You're a very caring, responsible alpha—"

"A little too responsible," Leo interjected, though he'd lost some of his ire. "Did you really intend on never taking a mate because of us?"

An awkward silence filled the room, the two of them watching me expectantly for an answer.

"It hasn't been high on my priority list." That was an understatement, but I didn't want them to feel responsible for my decision. Neither of them had ever outright said that I shouldn't take a mate—I'd made that choice on my own.

"I swear—I *swear*—that I will do every school drop off and pickup this week. I'll stay home every night. No fights, no going out. I'll be one hundred percent there for Freya, okay? Now, will you go?" Leo asked. "I'm not saying you have to make any other decisions right now, but the heat one should be easy."

"Should it?"

"Fuck yeah." He gave me a sidelong look. "She must have trusted you to ask you. And you must care about her to have considered it."

I grunted in agreement.

"Well, then, it's a no-brainer, isn't it? Unless you're fine with the idea of her in excruciating pain for five days, I guess."

I growled immediately, annoyed by how smug they both suddenly looked.

Dad pulled the phone out from under his ass, holding it out to me. "Call whoever you were talking to. Get it arranged. Leo, drive him up there— he's in no state to do it himself."

It was either going to be the best decision I'd ever made, or the worst. Maia answered on the first ring, her voice thick with relief when I said I was on my way as she assured me she'd call the agency and arrange for the support crew to meet me at the house.

Presumably, in normal circumstances, this would have all been set up with more notice, but I doubted they were going to say no to Inika Dara. There were definitely perks to her privilege.

Leo was more calm and focused than I'd seen him in years as he drove me to Mayfair. He didn't push me to talk about anything I didn't want to talk about, which I appreciated, but he did offer me some surprisingly insightful tips about omegas in heat that I shouldn't have been surprised by—he'd once been a mated alpha, after all—but I was.

It helped my brain stay on track. I could get Inika through these next five days—it would be a fucking honour to do so—but what happened on the other side of it was still very much a mystery. It sounded like my family was on board with me taking a mate, which I honestly hadn't expected them to be for some reason.

But that didn't clear all of the obstacles in our way. We still were who we were. The dire distance between our social classes still existed. We were two people from very different worlds who had a fucking incredible amount of sexual chemistry. But was that enough in real life? To actually *build* something together?

And then there'd been that conversation with her dad that I'd tried not to overhear, but had caught every word of anyway. It almost sounded like Inika *was* ready to give up some aspects of her lifestyle, if it meant that she had both freedom and privacy.

Those things I *could* offer her.

Maybe all hope wasn't lost then?

Focus, Blake. Just get her through her heat.

"Alright," Leo said, yanking up the hand brake as we stopped outside of Inika's home. "This is all you. Don't worry about anything else—we've got it taken care of. Just... well, be a good alpha."

I nodded once. "Thank you for the pep talk, I guess."

Leo smiled wryly. "I owe you a few. Go on. Good luck."

The moment I approached the front door, it was all a whirlwind. Stern-faced, mated alphas in dark scrubs frog-marched me into the reception room, grilling me on my willingness to be there.

A tired, nervous-looking beta who I assumed was Maia would occasionally appear in the doorway, watching for a while before vanishing somewhere else—presumably to check on Inika.

"What do I have to do to get this moving?" I barked. "I want to see Inika."

"Nearly done," Gerardo—who seemed to be the team leader said. "Do you understand that the muzzle can only be unlocked by one of us? When you need food or a break, you can leave the nest and one of us will remove it for you. It will be secured in place again before you return to the nest. Understood?"

"I understand," I replied impatiently. "Is someone asking Inika all these questions? I don't know for certain that she actually wants me here."

I thought I might die if she didn't.

"You'll know," Gerardo said drily, setting a leather case on the table and opening it up. "She is... instinct-driven at this point. A conversation wouldn't be productive, but she will certainly be able to let you know her opinion of you."

"Is she in her nest?"

Gerardo shook his head, pulling out an elaborate leather contraption that had to be the muzzle. "Generally, we wouldn't have agreed to providing assistance to an unknown alpha that the client hadn't even mentioned with basically no notice. However, Ms Dara is... well, she's showing signs of distress. She won't enter the nest at all."

Two of the alphas grabbed me by the arms, yanking me back as I made to head for the hallway.

"Muzzle on first," Gerardo said patiently, holding it out as he approached, careful not to trigger an aggressive response in me.

It was black, and made of a thick leather that I didn't particularly want wrapped around my face, but I'd do whatever I needed to do to get to Inika. A padded bit went between my teeth, while straps were secured in three spots behind my head—above the ears, below the ears, and behind the neck. It clicked into place as they locked it, and I supposed that I could take comfort in the fact that it definitely wasn't going to slip off by accident in the heat of the moment.

The leather bit between my teeth had a faintly bitter taste—just enough to discourage me from chomping down on it whenever the urge to bite struck. It was a primitive design in some ways, but it was incredibly effective.

"Come on, then. Let's see if you pass the omega's inspection."

Chapter 20

BLAKE

The only reason I hadn't smelled Inika from downstairs was that the ventilation system had been ramped up to its maximum setting. It meant the house was cold, but also that fresh air was being cycled through from outside constantly, not giving her scent a single second to linger.

But once we were upstairs, within a few feet of her... The scent of her perfume was undeniable. Not just her regular perfume, either.

The rut was calling to me like a siren song, begging for me to let go of the trappings of civilised society and to fuck her like a wild beast in her nest, the way she needed.

"Don't be offended if she rejects you—" Gerardo began, but before he could even finish that sentence, Inika was launching herself at me. She was wearing the same top and shorts I'd left her in this morning, though instead of hanging loosely off her frame, they were now glued to her skin with sweat.

I caught her easily, lifting her up, but before she could lean in to bury her face at my throat, a muzzle came down between us.

Fuck, they were quick.

I tightened my grip, a purr of reassurance rumbling out of my chest as Inika writhed, trying to escape the muzzle to no avail. It went fiercely against my own instincts not to help her get away from it, but I was holding on to just enough logic and reason to know that it had to be done.

Above all else, I didn't want either of us to walk out of that nest with regrets.

I glanced at Gerardo, who nodded once. "That's a pretty clear-cut acceptance, alpha."

That was all the encouragement I needed.

I took one step towards the spare room—the backup nest—but Inika immediately snarled in protest, tightening her thighs around me and urging me towards her *proper* nest. Which I supposed wasn't surprising, since we'd already been in there once before.

Gerardo made a sound of discontent. "This is all very unusual. There will need to be a full briefing about this afterwards—"

"That's not the priority right now," Maia snapped, hovering as far away as possible while still having us in her sight line. "You can contact me to arrange a meeting next week."

I couldn't speak, so I was glad that Inika was aware enough of her surroundings to reach for the door handle when we got to her nest so the biometric scanner could pick up her fingerprint.

I carried her inside the moment the door unlocked, and when it shut behind us, I felt like a thousand-pound weight had slipped off my shoulders.

Finally. It was just us.

It wasn't like all the other times I'd taken Inika to bed, though. She wasn't going to drop to her knees now in sweet submission, look up at me and wait for instructions, that was for fucking sure.

Inika wriggled out of my arms, ripping her clothes off her body like they offended her before turning her wild gaze onto my garments. I stripped off quickly and kicked everything aside, not wanting to risk her wrath.

I'd never seen an unmated omega in heat before. She was beautiful, sexy, and a little terrifying.

She herded me towards the nest, which gratifyingly still smelled like me, pushing me down into the centre and beginning the same process of arranging cushions around me as she'd done yesterday. It wasn't quite the same, though. There was more urgency this time. More frustration.

And a fuckton more slick coating my thigh as she straddled it, shamelessly grinding her clit on me with each movement she made.

I wanted to give her words, to encourage her, but I let my hands say what my mouth couldn't, reverently stroking every inch of her body I could reach.

The last thing I remembered before the rut took over was Inika riding my knot, scoring lines into my chest with her nails with each rock of her hips.

I snuck back into the room, freshly hydrated and with another dry protein bar sitting heavily in my stomach, getting reaccustomed to the muzzle as I slipped back into the sticky nest.

Inika immediately reached for me, throwing her leg over my waist and moving like she was going to climb on top of me, before wincing and pulling back, blinking up at me with bloodshot eyes.

The heat had broken.

I held myself still, not entirely sure how this next part was going to go. How cognisant had Inika been that *I* was the one in her nest?

She reached up with trembling fingers, delicately tracing the outline of the muzzle against my cheek.

As much as I wanted to give Inika time, the unsure look on her face was killing me. I scooped her up into my arms so she was laid on top of me, cuddling her close.

Was she okay? What was she thinking?

We needed to get these fucking muzzles off.

I was more exhausted than I'd ever been in my life, but the prospect of hearing Inika's voice again gave me a sharp shot of energy. I sat up with her on my lap, tugging one of the plum-coloured sheets free and wrapping around her as best I could. Inika helped with clumsy fingers, her head repeatedly lolling back against my shoulder.

I didn't know what happened now. Maybe she'd kick me out with a polite "thank you for your service." Or maybe she'd want me to stay. Either way, I was going to make sure that she got the rest, hydration, and sustenance she needed.

There was no point in me putting clothes on. I'd been wandering out of here—dick and balls on display—for the last five days, whenever my stomach felt like it was consuming itself and I had to eat something. The Prendre team had seen it all at this point.

"Ms Dara," Gerardo said instantly, not looking particularly surprised to see her, which I supposed meant that we were right on schedule. "We're going to release you both now."

He paused, watching me for a moment, presumably to see if I was going to put her down. Which I was not.

Two alphas approached with the small key chip things they inserted to release the muzzle, pulling both of ours off at the same time. The straps had left faint red lines over Inika's cheeks and jaw, and I traced them with my thumb, wanting to soothe them away.

Wasn't I meant to be taking it slow? Feeling out the situation and what Inika even wanted?

She was so pretty though. And her skin was so soft.

"Ms Dara?" Gerardo asked. "May I?"

She wordlessly stuck out her arm, still staring up at me, and it took me a moment to realise that he was pumping a syringe into her upper arm. Right, the postcoital contraception shot.

We were each handed water bottles, and I watched to make sure Inika drank at least half of hers before taking a sip of my own.

"Right, is everyone okay?" Gerardo asked in his military-style voice. "We've got a cooler of supplies here if you're going to head back into the nest to recover."

"I'm doing well," Inika said.

Her *voice*. There it was. I'd missed it so much. It didn't sound as full and vibrant as it usually did, but she had been moaning and whining through a muzzle for five days with very little sleep.

"Blake? Are you okay?"

"Of course."

"Let's nap in my nest," she said decisively, giving me an exhausted smile. I tucked the sheet a little tighter around her, carefully accepting the cooler that Gerardo handed me. If any of these alphas saw so much as a hint of her naked flesh, I might have to gouge out their eyeballs. "Thank you for everything. You guys can head out now, if you'd like," Inika added, as I carried her away, not giving them a chance to respond.

"It's okay if you want me to leave, princess. I won't be offended."

Inika glanced at me sharply. "I'm going to pretend you didn't just say that."

"Noted."

I did my best to suppress a smile. Sweet, relaxed, submissive Inika had completely left the building during her heat. There'd been no hesitation in demanding what she wanted, nor in letting me know with a dainty omega growl when I was taking too long to deliver.

Apparently, she was still feeling a little fired up. It was sexy as fuck. If my dick was capable of functioning, it'd be standing at attention.

Inika buzzed us into the room, and we both froze as the door sealed shut behind us, a shiver seeming to pass from her body to mine at the thick scent of *us* that permeated the room. It was... indescribable. My cock stirred valiantly, before retreating again. I needed a nap and something other than a protein bar in my stomach before I could even consider that.

I set Inika down on her feet and carried the cooler over to the small side table and chairs by the covered window. It was better than protein bars, but not by much. Grilled chicken. Grilled vegetables. Omelette. Avocado slices.

"Are you not allowed fun food post-heat?" I groused, opening the containers and setting them out on the tables.

Inika laughed, accepting the electrolyte drink I handed her. "Prendre always provides recovery foods. But I usually ask Graeme to send up something I actually want after I've slept for a bit."

"Oh yeah. With the alpha?" I asked, as casually as I could manage.

Inika raised an eyebrow at me. "No. Not with the alpha. This part I usually do on my own."

I hummed like that wasn't a massive relief, patting my thigh to encourage her to come and sit down. She dropped into my lap with a dramatic sigh, though, she somehow managed to make it look graceful.

"Drink some more," I ordered, nudging the bottle in her hand before making her a plate of tasteless nutrition.

"Been reading up on omega management?" Inika teased.

I snorted. "Actually, Leo—my twin—gave me a crash course on the drive over to your house. It didn't even occur to me to ask him, but I guess when it came to Ella, Freya's mum, he'd tried really hard to be a good mate."

Inika gave my hand a gentle squeeze, not offering me any useless platitudes which I appreciated. My complicated relationship with my brother was something I'd have to come to terms with on my own, but for the first time it seemed possible that we'd find common ground. Or maybe it was just the happy post-heat hormones making me see the world through rose-tinted glasses. Who knows if Leo had actually kept his word while I was away?

I was going to have to confront that, but I had some questions I needed to ask here first.

"What happens now?" I asked, nudging the bottle again.

Her lips twitched as she lifted it up, taking a sip. "What do you want to happen?"

Surely, it couldn't be that simple?

"I want to keep you."

Inika's expression didn't give much away, but her scent did. She liked that idea. I might have expired on the spot if she hadn't.

"You don't want a mate," she pointed out, her voice a little less certain this time.

I banded my arms tightly around her waist, keeping her close. "I didn't want a mate until I met you. I didn't see how I could make room for someone in my life until I saw you in it. To be honest, my family gave me a bit of a kick up the arse on that front. Maybe I was making sacrifices that no one had asked me to make."

"I'd never want to take you away from Freya, or the rest of your family," Inika said solemnly. "I adore Freya."

"She adores you too." I hesitated, rubbing my thumb restlessly over her thigh. "There's still... I don't know. Everything else, princess. We come from different worlds."

"So we do."

"I'm never going to fit in your world, Inika."

She leaned in to kiss my cheek. "I don't even fit in my world. And I won't fit entirely into yours either. But—perhaps I'm being naive—I kind of feel like if we have each other, we could tackle anything."

Inika adjusted her position so she could tuck her face into the crook of my neck. "I'm not saying it'll all be smooth sailing, but I am saying that it will be worth it."

"I think so too," I murmured, scarcely daring to breathe, afraid that this moment would slip between my fingers. "I love you. I think I have for awhile now."

"Oh, I know I've loved you for awhile, Blake Alwis." Inika nuzzled into my skin, sticky and sweaty and perfect. "We're going to be good together, right?"

"We're going to be amazing, princess."

Chapter 21

INIKA

I'd messaged Maia instructions from bed while Blake had coordinated with his family, so by the time we made it downstairs two days later—showered, dressed, mostly rested—it was to a beautiful breakfast and Blake's family sitting around the dining table.

"Inika, this is my dad, David, and my brother, Leo," Blake said, watching fondly as Freya threw her arms around my waist, hugging me like she hadn't seen me in years. "And Freya, you already know."

"I missed you," Freya said, squeezing me tightly.

"I missed you too, Freya. Shall we sit down and have some breakfast?"

Leo and David looked terribly uncomfortable, and I did my best to make small talk, asking how they liked their tea and pouring it for them in the hopes that I could make them feel more at ease.

Maia had arranged for a full English to be set out on the table, and I encouraged everyone to help themselves while piling food onto my own plate at Blake's insistence.

"You, uh, feeling alright then, Inika?" David asked, clearing his throat. "After your... Well. You know."

"Fine, thank you," I assured him, squeezing Blake's leg under the table as he choked on his tea.

"Is Uncle Blake your mate now?" Freya asked, which had the effect of making *all* the alphas start choking and spluttering.

"Well, no... Not yet."

"I'm her boyfriend," Blake interjected, looking oddly smug. It wasn't an expression I'd seen on him before, and it was adorable.

"Are you going to come and live with us, Inika?" Freya asked, before sitting up a little straighter in her seat. "Can we come and live with you? Your house is nicer."

"Frey..." David began uncomfortably.

"We wanted to talk to you about that," Blake interrupted. "Inika and I want a place that feels like a fresh start for both of us. For *all* of us. There are some fixer-uppers farther out, away from the city, that we could afford together."

I nodded. Blake wanted us to be as equal as possible, all things considered, and I absolutely respected that. And we both loved the idea of restoring a historic home to its former glory. Well, I could come up with ideas and he could do the restoring. At least in the short term. Eventually, I wanted to develop some more practical skills of my own.

"There's one we're particularly keen on looking at. It has plenty of room for all of you." Blake cleared his throat. "It actually has some outbuildings, which would give us all our own space. Which I think would be... beneficial."

"I want to live with Inika," Freya said, frowning.

"We'll figure out the details later, Frey," Leo said, looking between us. "Are you sure you wouldn't rather just have a fresh start, Blake? You took us in and I appreciate that. I, uh, know I haven't always made it easy on you."

"You haven't," Blake agreed bluntly. "But I think we're making progress. Don't you?"

Leo nodded, swallowing thickly.

"Might be good for you to get out of Streatham," David said quietly, looking at Leo. "Have a fresh start. Meet some different people."

Leo nodded glumly. "Schools and stuff, though…"

"There's a great school nearby," I offered quietly. "It's mixed, but popular among omegas, in particular."

"And we'll help you fix up the house of course," David said hastily. "I was a builder my whole life. We all know Blake's a top-notch plasterer. Leo's handy on the tools too, when he wants to be."

"I can help," Freya added, glaring at her grandfather for forgetting to mention her.

"And Frey is an excellent wee helper," David amended, lips twitching. "I don't want to count my chickens before they've hatched or anything, but I'm quite fond of the idea, all told. Blake has never taken much space for himself, and he ought to. He does so much for us." David ran a shaky hand through his grey hair. "I wish I could say don't you worry about me, I'll be just fine on my own."

"Absolutely not," Blake said firmly.

David shot him a sad smile. "I'm not sure I'd do too well on my own these days."

That wasn't an easy admission for an alpha to make, and I could see that it cost him. David rolled his neck, visibly uncomfortable, but Freya's omega instincts kicked in instantly. She carefully climbed onto his lap for a cuddle, taking a bit of toast with her and immediately decorating the front of her purple dress with crumbs.

"This is all a little... backwards," Leo said, looking between Blake and me. "Usually, the mating happens, *then* you figure out where to live and stuff."

Blake frowned. "Seems impractical. And Inika and I aren't twenty-year-olds with the world at our feet and plenty of time to figure it all out. We've got responsibilities. We've got other people depending on us."

"And we want to make this work," I added in a softer voice. "For everyone. We'd much rather take our time and do things right."

"Mum would have liked her," David grunted, not quite able to make eye contact with anyone as he tipped his chin at me.

"So would Ella," Leo said, though his tone was more wistful. Blake blinked in surprise. Perhaps Leo didn't talk about his late mate very often.

"Now that's sorted, can we enjoy our breakfast?" Blake asked, adding another piece of bacon to my plate. "I'm too tired for any more heavy conversations."

I smiled into my teacup, wishing I could remember my heat more clearly. I'd heard that some couples filmed the experience so they could watch it back later when the haze had cleared, but Brigitte had advised me not to do it. Apparently, some things couldn't be unseen.

"I can understand that," David laughed. "Sounds like you've squeezed in plenty of heavy conversations over the past couple of days."

I looked at Blake thoughtfully. "I think they were blunt conversations rather than heavy. We're not exactly spring chickens."

Blake grunted in agreement. "We don't want to waste a single minute."

It sounded more romantic when he said it.

"You're plenty young. Are you going to sit down with your parents?" David asked, pulling Freya's plate over towards him so she could stay on his lap and eat her breakfast.

"At some point. I've been asked to attend a meeting at my dad's company today. Presumably so they can tell me that I'm no longer in line to inherit it, as I didn't emerge with a mate."

"Not just any mate," Blake clarified, scowling. "The *right kind* of mate."

Leo laughed. "Your blood ain't blue enough for that."

"Not even a little," Blake agreed, his eyes on me. "But I love Inika. I don't think there's a single alpha on this planet who could love her better than me. If that's not good enough for her parents' approval, then I don't know what is."

"Hear, hear," I said, holding up my tea cup to him in toast.

The trouble was convincing them to *just* be my parents, just for this conversation at least. And that wasn't going to happen until I'd faced the board of Om-Guard.

"Do you want me to go in with you or wait out here?" Blake asked, his tone perfectly neutral, accepting my answer either way.

It would have been dishonest to pretend I hadn't emerged from my heat a little nervous about how this was going to go. Prior to this, I'd *liked* Blake— even toyed with the idea of being in love with him—but I'd also been acutely aware that we'd never had anything approaching a traditional relationship. What if we weren't actually compatible at all after all of that? What if he wanted to boss me around outside of the bedroom too?

But so far, those fears appeared to have been unfounded. Blake had gone out of his way to be conscientious, checking in on me constantly while somehow never talking down to me the way so many alphas did.

Blake simultaneously trusted that I knew my own mind and could make my own decisions, while babying me just enough to keep my heart in a puddle of gooey contentment. I wondered if he even knew he was doing it.

I exhaled shakily, giving his hand a quick squeeze. "I'll go in alone. This conversation has been a long time coming. I suspect Papa will want us to go to his house afterwards, though, so you can meet my parents."

"I want to meet them too."

I leaned over, pressing a kiss to his cheek as Brian stuck his head around the door, gesturing for me to enter while sparing a wary look in Blake's direction.

The nerves I'd expected never kicked in as I made my way into the meeting room, acutely aware of all the stares directed at my unmarked throat. I'd deliberately pulled my hair back and worn a scoop-necked top to make it easier for them—I wasn't hiding anything.

In fact, I felt more honest now than I'd ever felt in my life. Like I'd shed a too-tight skin that I'd been wearing since birth, revealing the true Inika underneath. Still a little spoiled, still a little out of touch, still fond of shiny things and expensive vacations.

But I was other things too. I always had been. I'd just kept them to myself because I'd thought I had to. Because wanting more—even if that *more* was in the form of new experiences—had seemed so greedy. So excessive. How dare I wish for anything beyond what I'd already been so blessed with?

I was still grateful for all of those things. But I was allowed to make choices for myself too.

"Inika," Samira said, gesturing for me to take the seat next to her. "It's good to see you."

It hadn't escaped my notice that Papa hadn't been the one to greet me. He was slumped in his seat, looking defeated. I was gracious enough to allow him some time to be disappointed, but I wouldn't give him forever to get over it. From what Mama had said, she wasn't my grandparents' first choice of mate for Papa, but he'd fought for her, and I would absolutely fight for Blake.

I would fight for *myself*.

"Hello everyone," I said, sitting down and surveying the room. "In the interest of getting the awkwardness out of the way, as you can see, I did not take a mate during my most recent heat."

Hans sighed heavily, folding his hands in front of him on the table, while Papa stared despondently at his laptop.

"While I have met the alpha I intend to take as my mate next year"—everyone perked up at that— "we have no intention of being involved with Om-Guard beyond my existing role at the company—if it's still available to me. I wish you all the very best with the succession planning, and I'm sorry I wasn't able to give you a firm answer on this subject before now."

I crossed my ankles and looked around expectantly. I'd done all the heavy lifting in this conversation, the least they could do was politely thank me for it.

"You're... quite sure this is what you want, Inie?" Papa asked quietly.

"Quite sure, yes."

"The product research team has no complaints about your performance, Inika," Olivier said gently. "In fact, the managers have repeatedly praised your efforts. I'm sure they will be more than happy to retain you if you still want the position."

"That would be great." I didn't know if I necessarily wanted to work there forever—I'd never considered any other kind of job because I'd always been so loyal to Om-Guard—but I was making enough big life changes as it was right now. It wouldn't be the worst idea to keep one thing the same.

"Well," said Hans after a lingering silence, clearing his throat uncomfortably. "That's probably all we needed to discuss with you, Inika."

"Excellent." I moved to stand, but Papa chose that moment to finally speak up.

"Inika, please wait. Let's wrap the meeting up for today, hm?" he said to the rest of the room. "We can resume the conversation later."

Everyone hurriedly packed up their things, eager to get out of the stifling boardroom. The omega urge to fuss and soothe was still there—I hadn't shaken it completely—but it wasn't as pressing as it usually was. Maybe because I was still so drained from my heat that I didn't have anything left to give.

Or maybe it was Blake. Either way, I wasn't going to question my good luck.

I startled as Samira's hand landed softly on my forearm, and she gave me a far kinder smile than the one she usually gave me. "I'm happy for you, Inika. You seem more... settled. Within yourself. Good for you."

"Thank you," I murmured, not particularly taking her words to heart. I'm sure Samira didn't have ill intentions, but it worked out in her best interests to have one less obstacle to deal with.

They all filed out of the room, and I did my best not to grin to myself at the thought of them walking past a scowling Blake in the hallway. Who knew what they'd make of him. I was confident that *he* wouldn't be impressed by *them*.

"Inie..." Papa began, closing his laptop and peering at me like he'd never seen me before. "Lately, I look at you and I feel like I don't know you anymore."

I nodded at that fair assessment. "I understand, Papa. The problem is that for a long time, I've been having that thought myself every time I looked in the mirror. I'm afraid that's no way to live."

Unlike our one-sided, unproductive dining table conversation a few days ago, he actually appeared to be listening to me this time. With no small amount of discomfort, I noted happily. It wasn't that I wanted him to suffer, but I did want him to *hear* me.

"All this time, I've been working towards a dream that I'm not sure was ever really mine. I never gave myself the space to consider what *my* dreams might be, because this was the path that was set for me and I followed it faithfully. And I still don't really know, but that's okay. Now I'm free to figure it out, without this predefined future hanging over my head."

"And the alpha you've chosen?" Papa asked. "You've never mentioned him before. I know it's not Hugo, I spoke to him on the phone during your heat and he reiterated what you'd said about there being no possibility there."

My eye twitched at that, and I took a few calming breaths before I said something I regretted. Papa made no apologies for that—he probably didn't even comprehend the fact that he'd completely steamrolled me, and I wasn't going to get into it today. Sometimes, I wasn't in the mood to gently educate full-grown alphas on the concept of other people having feelings.

"Blake is the alpha I have chosen, and I love him," I replied simply. "In all of the dreams I have for my future, he's right there with me."

For all Papa's flaws—and I wasn't feeling overly forgiving about them at the moment—he finally managed a tentative smile. "Well, I better meet him, then. But not without Mama—she'll never forgive me otherwise."

"Come to my house for dinner," I suggested, though there wasn't much room for negotiation in my voice. I infinitely preferred the option of having them come to a space that Blake was familiar with for this encounter rather than us going to them. "You can meet Blake and we'll show you the home we're looking at purchasing together."

I lifted my chin, daring him to disagree. I was thirty-four years old. I'd spent my entire life doing what was expected of me, and I wasn't about to do it for another second more.

"I'll go home and get Mama, and we'll see you soon."

BLAKE

"Are you sure you've got the Fontaine job under control?" I asked Leo as we drove home after work, Freya sitting in the seat between us, elbow-deep in a bag of crackers that was probably turning her white school uniform shirt orange.

"Yes," Leo replied, exasperated. "We're leaving all the decorative stuff until you're back on board anyway, and we built your ten days off into the project scope. Stop stressing, Blake."

"Aunty Inika says stressing isn't good for your heart, Uncle Blake," Freya added serenely before shoving another handful of crackers into her mouth.

"You can remember that but you can't remember to wear your tie to school."

Freya shrugged, unbothered, while Leo watched her affectionately. For now, she lived in the main house with Inika, Dad, and I, while Leo was on his own in the outbuilding we'd done up a few feet from the big house. Freya had a bedroom there too, and she'd probably spent most of next week there while

Inika and I retreated to the nest, but the current arrangement suited us all just fine for now.

Freya had needed consistency, and Leo had needed time and space to sort his head out. This setup had given us both. Freya had been excelling at her new school—with the exception of all the uniform infractions she'd received—and Leo had been going to grief counselling and showing up to work with me each day.

It wasn't perfect, but it was better than it had been in years. We had Inika to thank for that.

She came out to meet us as we pulled up in front of the house, still looking like my expensive city girl in her dark blue skirt and matching loose crop top, though the knee-high yellow wellington boots were a country touch.

"One of you needs to get your father off the ladder right now," she said the moment we opened the van doors. "He's insisting on changing the lightbulb by the back door."

"On it," Leo said, jogging around the house while I waited by the driver's door, accepting all the things Freya was handing me to carry inside.

"Did you have a good day, princess?" I asked, leaning down to kiss Inika as she sidled up next to me, immediately reaching up to massage the back of my neck.

"I did. I got lots of work done, and I ripped out the carpet in the spare bedroom."

I snorted, wrapping an arm around her waist. "Of course, you did."

I hadn't actually expected Inika to be so hands-on when it came to the renovation, but it turns out that she found the destruction of property quite therapeutic.

Her friends had found that a little baffling, but they'd been baffled by most of Inika's life choices in the past year. It had made for an odd few months, but they seemed to be finding a new normal now. Brigitte had come out to visit for the day just last week, and she'd very thoughtfully brought Freya a birthday present.

"You're warm," I murmured as Freya jumped down from the car, blowing Inika a kiss before running into the house. She was usually very affectionate with her, but she seemed to have picked up that Inika couldn't tolerate a lot of physical contact at the moment from anyone except me.

"Mmhm. You ready, alpha?"

"I've been waiting all year to get my bite on you. Of course I'm ready."

"Good." Inika sighed dreamily. "I can't wait."

"Come here, omega," I growled, infusing my voice with alpha command as my desperate little omega leaned back in the shower, rubbing her clit like she'd die if she didn't. She was still somewhat lucid—aware, at least, that she wanted to wash the scent of the outside world off her before she climbed into her nest—but very much fixated on pleasure.

But her pleasure was my job.

Inika walked into the towel I was holding out for her, pressing her wet face against my throat and purring contentedly as I patted her skin dry. Fuck, she smelled heavenly.

"Did you eat?" I asked. She nodded against my skin, tugging in frustration at the towel, hating the feel of the material against her skin when she was already so sensitive. I tossed it aside, scooping her up into my arms and stepping over the clothes I'd already discarded, carrying her back to the nest.

My gums ached, the anticipation of a full year of waiting thrumming in my veins, but it was too early for that. It wasn't safe to place the mating bite until the heat had fully set in.

I dropped Inika on the edge of the bed, cupping her face gently and staring into her eyes.

"Roll over, my pretty little slut. Let's see how slick that cunt is for me."

The coppery tang of blood filled my mouth. It wasn't pleasant, and yet somehow, it was the best thing I'd ever tasted. My omega clenched around my knot, arching back into my bite with a whine.

Mine.

"Are you awake?" Inika rasped, her voice clear though tired after five intense days.

I hummed, eyes too heavy to open, squeezing her a little tighter where she lay on top of me.

"We're mated," she whispered, smiling against my chest.

"Fuck, I hope so. I'd have been annoyed if I'd waited all year and then forgotten to bite you."

Inika shook with laughter. "I doubted I would have let you get away with that, alpha."

"Mm, I doubt that too," I agreed, reaching down to massage the globes of her ass. My memories of the past five days were pretty hazy, but Inika hadn't been shy and retiring in any of them. "No regrets, princess?"

"Not a single one. What about you?"

I forced my eyes open as Inika propped her head up on her hands, peering down at me. "Absolutely not. I'm so in love with you, Blake."

"I'm so in love with you too. I'm going to show you that every single day for the rest of our lives."

ACKNOWLEDGEMENTS

THANK YOU ALL FOR TAKING A CHANCE ON THIS SERIES. ON THE SHELF IS A BIT OF A SANDBOX FOR ME—IT'S WHERE I PLAY AROUND WITH SLIGHTLY DIFFERENT TROPES AND PUSH MYSELF A LITTLE OUTSIDE OF MY WRITING COMFORT ZONE. THIS ONE WAS VERY SMUT&VIBES, AND I HAD AN ABSOLUTE BLAST WORKING ON IT. I HOPE YOU ENJOYED IT TOO X

THANK YOU TO MARCELLE AT BOOKS CHECKED FOR PUTTING UP WITH ME, YOU DESERVE A MEDAL, HONESTLY <3

COLETTE XX

ABOUT THE AUTHOR

Colette Rhodes is a paranormal romance author from New Zealand. She loves to write about love in all its forms, and adores imperfect heroes and heroines who find perfection in each other. You'll often find her trying to justify her degree by including ancient history and mythological influences in her work.

If she's not writing, then you're almost certain to find her reading—ideally with a cup of tea in hand and a scented candle burning to match the mood.

Keep up with Colette here:

coletterhodes.com

@coletterhodes_author

ALSO BY COLETTE RHODES

SHADES OF SIN:

Luxuria

Superbia

Gula

Avaritia

Invidia

Ira

Acedia

STATE OF GRACE:

Run Riot

Silver Bullet

Wild Game

Dare Not

Saving Grace

THREE BEARS DUET:

Gilded Mess

Golden Chaos

LITTLE RED DUET:

Scarlet Disaster

Seeing Red

ON THE SHELF:

Scheme

Excess

KNOTTY BY NATURE:

(omegaverse with T.S. Snow)

Allure Part 1

Allure Part 2

EMPATH FOUND:

The Terrible Gift

The Unwanted Challenge

The Reluctant Keeper

DEADLY DRAGONS:

The (Not) Cursed Dragon

The (Not) Satisfied Dragon

STANDALONE:

Dead of Spring (MF - Hades & Persephone retelling)